THE

SAD

PART

WAS

TRANSLATED BY

THE SAD PART WAS

PRABDA YOON

MUI POOPOKSAKUL

TILTED AXIS PRESS

ปลง **Ploang**

To put something down, to unburden, to be at peace with letting go. The last definition is the most common and the most significant. To *ploang* is a Buddhist approach for dealing with adversities and disappointments. It is not to dwell on something that causes suffering, nor is it to forget about it; it is learning to live, stoically, with it – a Thai recipe for contentment, an attitude that would place the emphasis on the last word in this collection's title.

PEN IN PARENTHESES

The sheet of paper fell (It's from a notebook I had when I was in seventh grade. Its blue lines are starting to fade. There's only a single sentence on the entire page, three lines down from the top. My handwriting was neat, done with a black ballpoint pen, and the letters are still surprisingly sharp. The sentence says: "I will never change."

Change from what, I can't remember anymore. I'm at a loss trying to figure out whether I've kept my own word. I'm trying to recall what I might have been thinking when I was about twelve or thirteen; whatever it was, it seems to have been a matter of life and death. Serious enough, at least, that I'd felt the need to promise myself not to deviate from whatever path I'd been on. Whatever idea I'd managed to dream up, I must have been really taken with it.

Philosophical aphorisms used to fascinate me, perhaps because I fancied myself as a wit. Maybe I happened to read something that really struck a chord with me, and decided to make it my mantra. There was one that went: "If you want to be a good person, that means you aren't." I slapped my knee after I read that: *Clever! Aha! That hits the nail right on the head. It's so true: wanting something means you still haven't achieved it. Therefore, I mustn't want it. Instead, I have to behave in such a way that other people will consider me to be good.* That one still cracks me up even now.

My mother said:

When you grow up, there might be a time when you ask yourself why you were put on this earth. When you can't find a reason, you'll blame your father and me for giving birth to you. 'I never begged you to bring me into this world. The two of you made an executive decision, and I wasn't even consulted.' I want to tell you right now that your father and I are sorry. What you're thinking is true. We had no right to give birth to you without asking. Not only did we bring you into this world, we boss you around, make you go to school, make you eat vegetables, make you read, make you get up, make you go to bed. We try to dictate your life. 'You should do this for a living. You should marry that kind of person. You have to wai these people nicely when you see them. You have to respect this person, call so-and-so uncle and so-and-so aunt.' Your father and I sincerely take the blame for all of this. If possible, when you feel like having a child of your own, ask it first if it wants to be born. If you

don't receive an answer, you can take that as a no. And if it
doesn't want to be born, don't bring it here. Let it be born to
a cat or a dog as fate will have it. Your father and I are sorry.
If you're angry or if you hate us, that's up to you.

My mother was smart. She said those things to
atone for her sins before she departed. After my parents
died in a car crash, all I could do was miss them. How
could I be angry at them or hate them? Just as I didn't
ask to be brought into this world, they didn't ask to be
plucked from it. At least, they wouldn't have wanted
to leave together, in the same instant. One of them
must have wanted to hang around for a bit, to stay
with me just a little while longer.

After the accident, my friends all worried that I
would turn into a troubled kid. But that wasn't the
case at all. I may have been sad that my parents weren't
with me anymore, but I was the type that has their
own universe, and it was large enough for me. The
external world with parents and friends was just that
– external. One or two people missing there didn't
cause *my* universe to crumble. Naturally, there were
times when I had to emerge from my world, and that
could leave me feeling sad and lonely. But it wasn't
enough of a big deal to make me turn to drugs or
have suicidal thoughts. Why would I? My world had
unlimited freedom. I could do anything I wanted, be

anything I wanted, eat anything I wanted, have all the fun in the world without worrying about anything. If I starting taking drugs, I would distance myself from that magical world. If I committed suicide, I would never get to revel in it again.

I thought about killing myself once when I was a kid. I was feeling sorry for myself after my father wouldn't buy me a plastic robot, even though it was way cheaper than the bottle of wine he'd just got for himself. I went and got one of his neckties from his wardrobe and looped it around my neck. In tears, I announced that I was going to hang myself. It was such a well-acted, award-worthy performance that I can still picture the scene to this day. Unperturbed, my father glanced at me briefly before walking away. *After you die,* he said, *please don't forget to call.* I didn't have any income of my own in those days. I didn't even have any change in my pockets, never mind a mobile phone. Even if the other world turned out to have pay phones, placing a call would probably have been beyond me.

Pay phones don't exist in the world of the dead, I'm sure of it now, because if they did, my parents would have called me as soon as they crossed over. I don't think they would have baulked at the cost.

After the accident, I moved in with my maternal grandparents. By the time I was born, my father's parents were already in the other world. My father told me that his father had been a lawyer. That was all I knew. I didn't know anything about his mother, other than what I could deduce for myself: she was a lawyer's wife. Once you have "wife" in your title, it doesn't make much of a difference whether you're a doctor's wife, a teacher's wife, or a janitor's wife. At the end of the day, even a snake's wife is there to serve her husband. No matter how tired she might be, the wife needs to have dinner ready on the table for when the snake comes home. If the snake's muscles are stiff, the wife has to give him a massage. If the snake is thirsty, he can't be expected to fetch water for himself.

My mother's father ran a congee shop in the market. Her mother was unusual in that she wasn't just a congee vendor's wife, she was also a teacher. She taught music at an elementary school. Her taste in music was also unusual: when I woke up in the morning, I used to hear Mozart, Beethoven, Bach. My grandmother liked to listen to loud music, much to the neighbours' annoyance. The young guy across the street was not to be shown up – he blasted out old-time rock and roll music every morning, giving my grandmother a run for her money. She would complain under her breath: *What the heck is this crazy music? I only hear nonsensical screaming and yelling. There's no artistry, no sustained harmony to please the senses.* But for other people in that neighbourhood, my grandmother was the odd one out, living in a wooden house surrounded by mango trees and hanging orchids, yet listening to the light-haired farangs' classical music. It just didn't make any sense around here.

When he wasn't selling congee, my grandfather was passionate about movies. He even shelled out for a 16mm projector, obtained from God knows where. Every Friday night, he sat his wife and grandson down and screened a movie of his choice. It was an important ritual for him. On a Friday when he was in a festive mood, he'd round up his friends to come spend the evening in front of the screen with us. Some of them focused on the movie; others focused on getting drunk, each to his own liking.

My grandfather's makeshift screen was a white bedsheet stretched tightly around the edges of a door. His projector didn't produce any sound, so my grandmother volunteered as the music director. Mozart was her eternal favourite. No matter what the movie was, the soundtrack had to be Mozart. To this day, whenever I watch a movie in a cinema, I can still hear the faint strains of Mozart echoing in my ears.

The film my grandfather screened most often was *Dracula*, the black and white version starring Bela Lugosi. If it was pouring outside when Friday came around, there was no need to wonder which movie he'd choose to suit the weather. Come to think of it, he even resembled Lugosi's Count Dracula. His cheeks were sallow, his eyes were sunken, and he wore his hair combed flat to his head; his jaw narrowed sharply to the point of his chin, while his jet-black eyebrows slanted up toward his temples. The only difference was that he didn't have fangs, and I never spotted any tell-tale puncture wounds around the base of my grandmother's neck. My grandfather was just an ordinary congee seller. However he was in the daytime, he stayed that way at night. He didn't turn into a bat and start flapping around terrorising people. He didn't get agitated and cover his face whenever he clapped eyes on a clove or two of garlic; he'd as soon as wolf it down. He was a Buddhist. He prayed to Buddha every night, right before his head hit the pillow. If someone took two long pieces of wood and arranged them into the shape of a cross, he wouldn't have batted an eyelid. And he loved the sun. In his spare time, he liked to squat down in the front yard to trim the grass, not bothering with a hat to shield his skin from the baking heat. Whereas if he were a vampire, his body would have burned to ashes the moment he stepped out of the door.

My grandfather was human, which meant he didn't possess eternal life. And so, one day, he died.

He used to say:

Dracula *isn't technically a ghost movie. Count Dracula is not some vengeful, disembodied spirit like those ghosts that have their guts ripped open, eyes rolled back, and tongues hanging out. He doesn't have supernaturally long arms like a certain infamous Thai ghost that dropped a lime into the basement and was too lazy to run down and get it. Dracula is simply an unfortunate soul: he cannot die. He is cursed with eternal life, condemned to live like a beast. We ought to pity him, really. The Count might not actually want to harm anyone. He would probably be perfectly happy just living in his beautiful castle, on top of a hill in Transylvania, and minding his own business. Having to transform into a bat and go after people's necks is probably not something that brings him joy. He can't even go to the mall in broad daylight like other people. We are truly lucky to be able to die when our time comes. Mortality is our most valuable asset.*

Nonetheless, after my grandfather proved that he, too, possessed this most valuable asset, I came to feel that immortality exists among humans as well. When someone dies, no matter who they are, they move into another person's body, and so on in endless succession, until the last human on earth disappears.

When my grandfather died, he moved into my grandmother's body. Every Friday she pulled out the white bedsheet and stretched it over the door, took the movie projector out of the closet and screened my grandfather's old movies to a captive audience: me. My grandmother became a person who had two souls in one body, in charge both of projecting the movie and arranging the soundtrack.

The film she screened most often was *Dracula*, with Mozart as the soundtrack. She usually alternated between Violin Concerto Number 5 (the "Turkish") and Symphony Number 41 (the "Jupiter"). These particular pieces didn't always fit very well with the pace and mood of the movie, but my grandmother's personal preference was always the deciding factor.

Everything proceeded as it always had, save for one person's breathing.

I lived with my grandmother until I went to university. She never interfered with my education: *Study whatever you want to study. Grandma doesn't know a thing about it.* She stopped teaching music a few years after my grandfather's passing. The congee shop stayed in business. The taste was a little different, but the customers still packed the place out. My grandfather's employees worked as diligently as ever, and even helped make sure that my grandmother was comfortable without becoming a burden to me. For my part, I carried on with my young and reckless life as normal.

I decided to study art because most of my friends were artists. Since I was no good at studying anything else, I acted like I was an artist, too. My drawings were pretty nonsensical, but luckily drawings with much sense in them are no longer in fashion. I used to believe that I was Picasso reincarnated. Later, I realised that even if I really were the second coming of Picasso, that wouldn't make any difference in the long run. If Picasso was an art student today, he'd probably flunk the course. The professors would say he was stuck in the past, that his stuff was old-fashioned. Why waste time drawing strange, hideous pictures? Nowadays, it isn't enough to just sit there sketching nudes. You have to think deep. You have to have a "concept."

So my friends were all into concepts. All they did each day was wander beyond the school walls to scavenge for concepts. If they didn't find any, no one complained. Inability to find a concept could be a concept in itself, so in that sense, bothering to scout around for one was a waste of time and energy.

In the four years that I spent doing art, I could count the number of concepts that I found on less than half a finger (what I did find being so lame an excuse for a concept, it didn't deserve the full digit). I couldn't even define the word "concept." The whole idea was beyond me. It's a miracle that I even found any. I was in awe of people who found a lot of them. Some students repeatedly borrowed other people's concepts. The professors didn't object – borrowing could be counted as a concept, too. In the end, I decided that a person's concept was the same as their "business concern." If other people found your "concern" interesting, you'd go places in life. If you didn't know how to come up with your own particular "concern," that's, well, your concern.

In the world beyond the school fence, you couldn't survive on your concern alone. If you wanted to make a fistful of cash, you had to put other people's concerns first. My friends who were so darn good at concocting their concerns scattered and then dealt with other people's – helped them sell shampoo, alcohol, chips, air-conditioners, clothes, tape, this and that, too many different things to enumerate. For some, it was a chore; for others, the more they sold, the more pride they took in their skill as sellers, which became a concept in and of itself. My grandfather was good at selling congee, but there was never any concept in it for him.

I fell into the same kind of lifestyle. As they say, when in Rome... Or as the Thai expression goes: when among the half-blind, keep one eye closed. So I went along with the others, squeezing one eye tight shut. These days, I can hardly see anymore. But I put up with it. When everyone else is busy turning a blind eye, who would notice if I managed to coax my inner Picasso out?

My friends and I graduated from an institution that happened to have alumni who were expert squinters, movers and shakers in many fields. So getting a job wasn't difficult. Even before graduation, we got recruited to go and do this and that, so we had early training in seeing with only one eye. The day after I got my diploma, I was already hanging out at the office that swiftly became my new address. I must say, my office was a glamorous place. I felt my own importance grow bit by bit just from sitting there. People around the office looked sharp. They wore clothes that were expensive, or at least ostensibly so. Everyone's hair was fashionably styled. Some people had perfectly good eyes – not nearsighted or farsighted or astigmatic – but still wore super thick black-rimmed glasses because that was a cool look. Geek chic, in its own way. Maybe, among the one-eyed, wearing glasses is a must. It was perfectly possible.

It turned out to hold true for me as well. I hadn't been sitting there for more than a few months when the bridge of my nose acquired a concern of its own: supporting a pair of black-rimmed glasses. My confidence immediately shot up. Whenever anybody asked, I said my eyes had started playing tricks on me, my vision deteriorating all of a sudden. I didn't know if I was nearsighted or farsighted, but I knew for sure that I couldn't see very clearly. In particular, my sight was suspiciously blurry when asked to focus on the products that I was supposed to promote. I didn't consult any doctors. I just decided to buy my own glasses. It was more of a psychological matter. When I wore them, my view of the world was clearer. It was easier to work with them on. I was better at selling. People showed respect and called me *pi*. For the first time, I experienced what it's like to have someone address you as pi when you're not their actual big brother. It put me on a high horse. My chest was mysteriously pumped up. But sometimes I had to hold those feelings in, not flaunt them in other people's faces. I had to feign humility, saying: *There's no need to call me pi. We're not far off in age.* But in my head I'd be saying: *If you don't fucking call me pi next time we run into each other, I'm done with you.* I would always remind those in my inner circle not to rely too much on the words that came out of my mouth. My words weren't straight, no matter which brand of ruler you used to draw the lines. It's in the nature of those used to turning a blind eye: their visual impairment causes their brain to twist their words, too. Don't hold it against our kind.

The first commercial that I created myself from behind my new glasses brought me moderate fame. As a welcome consequence, my social circle acquired several new *nongs* who practically begged to be treated as my little siblings. Another good thing that came out of it was the work that was pouring in. My work traded on humour. The more I made people laugh, the faster I advanced. I didn't care whether the product I had to sell was in any way related to the commercial I created. Luckily, neither did the product owners. In fact, the less the commercial had to do with the product, the better. As long as the brand name stuck in people's heads, I was on target. If you elaborated on the product's qualities, you might end up having to lie. Why risk going to hell for something that wasn't necessary? Just a little white lie would do, enough to create a buzz. Bees are tiny; no matter how much buzz they generate, the result remains inconsequential in the grand scale of things. When I worked, I thought of myself as a bee. But when I came up with a good sting, I was a lion.

My grandmother aged over time. I was hardly ever free to go and visit her. On the phone, she always sounded sprightly. Early every morning, she went to exercise in the park nearby with other friends her age. Whenever she had some free time, she didn't let it go to waste. She volunteered to babysit friends' kids and grandkids during the day, when she played her beloved classical music as lullabies for the children and herself. I knew she was strong both physically and emotionally, so there was no need for me to worry about her. But to tell you the truth, sometimes I was so preoccupied with myself that I plain forgot all about her, just eliminated her from my brain, like a dried leaf plucked off a plant. What an odd, ugly image. As if my grandmother were a shriveled leaf that no amount of sunlight could revive, a leaf that could no longer be fed, a withered leaf that ought to be trimmed off to make room for a fresh new bud. I had to remind myself constantly not to treat people like old leaves, especially my grandmother. If I tore her off, I'd be the only leaf left on the entire tree.

Some weeks ago, I got assigned to a new project. This time the product was breath mints. I was tossing ideas around in my head to see what I could dream up, and then the proverbial light bulb flicked on, as it does each time I crack a problem at work. I should point out that when I'm not thinking about work, no light bulb ever appears above my head. This must mean that my brain is otherwise dark and cloudy – it just blindly feels its way around and lets random thoughts wander. To find light each time, there's got to be a condition attached. If it's not for work or money, it just stays in the dark. The fear is, if the light's too bright, it might illuminate a shockingly hollow space. The repository of my brain might appear large from the outside, as if it contained an enormous supply of intelligence, but if a bright light bulb were shining in there all the time, you'd see an empty warehouse, pin-drop quiet. Better just to leave it in the dark.

This time, though, the lightbulb above my head illuminated the face of Bela Lugosi, made up as he is in the *Dracula* movie. That's it: I would find a guy with a pointy chin and have him dressed up to look like the Count. A mature actor past his prime would be best, someone who was having trouble landing any film or TV roles. I could chalk it up as an act of charity. Maybe the actor would make a comeback off the back of my commercial. Then I would become known as a savior who can bring the dead back to life, a person of great abilities. In the land of the one-eyed, age commands respect, even in a person who'd been consigned to the scrap heap only a few years earlier.

After I found my Count, I would need a model to play the unfortunate victim. A fresh-faced girl would be best, not one who's been made up for so many cameras that her pores have become clogged and her skin pimpled. That kind are all pop singers by now, anyway. It was too much fuss and too much money to secure them for a commercial. The best solution would be just to pick someone off the street. If the girl got lucky, her career might explode, and within a few months she might have turned into the next It Girl. And the luck wouldn't all be one way; if she was into older guys, I could take advantage of having introduced her to the industry and acquire some bare-ly-legal arm candy, if only for a few months. Once I'd found a female model to my liking, I would need a handsome male model to play the vampire slayer. The client would be happiest with someone already fairly famous. For me, it didn't matter either way. I wasn't after a handsome male model to hang on my arm. Let the gay guys on the team decide.

My commercial would have to be black and white, like the original film. The title would be in that Gothic-looking font often used for the opening credits of horror flicks. I would have huge letters reading, "Dracula Meets …" (The ellipsis was the brand name of the breath mint.) The first shot would be the Count's stone castle, perched on top of a hill. There's a torrential downpour. Lightning strikes with hair-raising flashes. From there we cut to the interior of the castle. Things are heating up between Dracula and the female victim, reclining on his bed. Then a close-up of the sharp tip of his fang moving in on the pale, smooth skin of her neck.

Suddenly, the Count hears the castle door being knocked down. Caught off guard, he pauses before he can sink his teeth into the young woman's neck and satisfy his craving. Cut to the bottom of the staircase on the ground floor of the castle, where the strapping young vampire slayer is mounting the stairs one at a time, a flaming torch in his left hand and a cross in his right. The Count appears out of nowhere at the top of the staircase. His face is boiling with rage. The young man doesn't hesitate. He throws the torch at Dracula, hoping to burn the vampire into submission. But the Count is a former kick volleyball player. Just one bounce off his head and the torch is deflected back onto the young slayer, who struggles to put out the fire burning his clothes. But the young man doesn't back down. Even though his hair is burnt to a crisp, he is determined to defeat the demon. Holding the cross up in front of him, he inches closer to the Count, but Dracula stands his ground, completely unfazed by the holy symbol. He even smirks, making a mockery of the young warrior. The handsome young man is genuinely baffled. Dracula abruptly takes pity on him and decides to reveal his secret. He gestures for the young man to turn around and look at the castle wall.

The camera pans to where the Count is pointing. Not far from the scene of their showdown, a shrine of Buddha images comes into view, complete with candles, incense and lotus flowers. Dracula has changed religion. Even a truck full of crosses would be of no use. Mortified, the young man breaks into a sweat and throws the cross aside. He puts his palms in prayer to wai the Count before bolting down the stairs and out of the castle gate. The scene cuts back to the Count's bedroom. The female victim is still lying motionless on the soft mattress. Dracula enters the room with a smile, ready to resume his attack. Cut to a close-up of the Count's fang once again. This time, when the sharp tip is about to graze her pale skin, the beautiful young woman opens her eyes and hands the vampire a breath mint. "If you don't suck on … you can't suck on me." (The ellipsis, again, being the brand name of the aforementioned breath mint.) And then she smiles sweetly. Dracula submissively pops the breath mint in his mouth.

The last shot is back outside the castle. The rain has stopped. It's becoming light out. Two bats fly out from the second-floor window, flapping jauntily side by side. The accompanying voice-over says, "The modern Dracula takes ..." (Ellipsis, breath mint.) After the two love-bats disappear offscreen, the words "Stay tuned for part two" appear – just in case this commercial of mine turned out to be a hit and the client commissioned me for a follow-up. If not, it didn't matter; it would still look cool, anyway.

The soundtrack would be sure to feature Mozart, but only as a faint background to the action. The main music would be the kind of formulaic stuff typical of horror movies, because in truth, Violin Concerto Number 5 and Symphony Number 41 didn't really chime with the content. But since I was selling my childhood memory, I might as well recreate it as closely as possible.

As I had guessed, my idea was well-received by the others in the office. I cooked it up for people to like, so it's natural that they did. That's what I do. It got the green light after just two meetings. We could start shooting right away.

They say we humans use only a tiny fraction of our brains. Those genius types might manage a little more than ordinary folks. But I'm no genius. The more I think, the smaller the fraction of my brain I use. And the bosses use an even smaller fraction than I do. Otherwise they wouldn't take to my shallow ideas so readily. Whatever I come up with leaves them in stitches. The lamer the idea, the louder they laugh.

The exploitation of my childhood memory was a success. The girl who played Dracula's victim didn't become my arm-candy, but I did get a round-eyed intern to take in the nightlife with me. We went sightseeing everywhere there was to see, after which there was no more seeing to be done, not even of each other. I have to start saving again to prepare for new sightseeing adventures with a new girl. Right now, I don't know who she's going to be, but that's nothing to get worked up about.

The Dracula Meets the Breath Mint commercial was a source of considerable pride for me. I even recorded it for my grandmother to watch when she got lonely.

I delivered the Dracula videotape to her in person, in a new car earned with my own blood, sweat, and tears. I had to have something to show off to drag myself over there. My grandmother was so happy. She spent the whole morning preparing my favorite foods so she could spoil me. I didn't waste a second when I got there. *Grandma,* I told her, *look at this first. I don't know if you've already seen it on TV. I made this commercial especially for you and Grandpa.* I pushed the videotape into the player. Excited, my grandmother waited eagerly for the picture to appear on the screen. But her screen wasn't the one on the TV. Her eyes were fixed on me, on my face, as if I were an old movie she hadn't seen in a long time. I pretended not to notice. I was busy mouthing off, giving her the behind-the-scenes story of the making of the commercial, not paying attention to whether or not she understood the advertising jargon. My grandmother didn't seem to mind either. She just sat and listened, eager and obedient. She smiled at whatever I said. When I laughed, she laughed. If all of my clients were like her, life would be great. Work would be so much easier.

My grandmother watched my Dracula Meets the Breath Mint commercial with a smile. But I felt strange watching it with her in her house, the setting of my memory of the blood-sucking Count, the memory that had earned me money to spend, that had bought me the vote of confidence from colleagues and clients.

I stared absentmindedly at my grandmother's ancient television set.

It's good, son, was her comment after the movie ended.

It's no good.

I asked if she heard the Mozart in the movie. She looked surprised: *Was Mozart in there?* I nodded: *Yes, the "Turkish" and the "Jupiter", the ones you always played as the soundtrack for* Dracula. *The one with Bela Lugosi, that Grandpa used to screen on Friday nights.* She said: *Oh yeah? Really? Was it there? I didn't hear it. I'm old, sweetheart. My hearing's not what it was.* I wanted to rewind the tape and show the movie to her again: *Grandma, listen closely.* She said: *There's no need. I believe that Mozart is in there, just like you said. We don't have to watch it again.*

Today I'm at my grandmother's house, but she is no longer here. I don't know where she's gone, just as I don't know where my parents have gone, or where my grandfather's gone. I came to my grandmother's house to pack up. Since my grandmother is no longer here, the house is no longer necessary. I came to go through the stuff and pick out anything I want to keep. I'm only realising now that my grandmother was quite the hoarder: school books, cartoons, magazines, toys, stuff from my childhood. She kept all of them neatly arranged in the cupboards. I probably can't take them all today.

There are dozens of boxes of my grandmother's classical music records, every one of them still in good condition. My grandfather's movie projector, too, is shiny as new. All of his movies are still in their metal cases. I held one of them in my hand for longer than the rest. The case was labelled "Dracula", in English, in my grandfather's handwriting. I thought of that white bedsheet and the beam of light from the projector, how it used to cut a line through the darkness on its way to the white fabric.

I flipped through several high school notebooks and textbooks with outdated-looking covers. They were full of doodles that I'd done surreptitiously during class. Many pages of the notebooks were smeared with Star Wars. I haven't played Star Wars in ages. It's a kid's game. You draw an army of stars and then you shoot a line with the tip of a ballpoint pen to try and hit the other player's army. Any star you hit gets blacked out.

I remember how I made several attempts to keep a diary, but got tired of it and gave up in less than a week each time.

What's there to record from a day in the life of a child, anyway? *Today I woke up and went to school. I got spanked by the teacher. I came home, watched TV, read some comics, went to bed.*

The sheet of paper with the faded blue lines is a page from one of the diaries I didn't finish.

"I will never change."

Change from what, I can't remember anymore.

But I want to keep it. Maybe I'll remember one day.), so I bent down and picked it up.

EI PLOANG

I don't have all that much to be proud of, but one memory that still makes me smile to this day is Ei Ploang calling me a good person.

I used to address him more politely as *Khun* Ploang; the bold switch to Ei is only a recent development, and one I never would have had the audacity to make without the express permission of the man himself.

One morning in Lumpini Park, Ei Ploang handed me a scrap of paper. "You can call me 'Ei' from now on," he said, "Here's a letter of certification." It even had a signature.

I opened the letter:

On the 17th of August 1999, I, Mr. Theppitak Rakakart (nickname Ploang), came, by destiny, to meet a young Thai man by the name of Praj Preungtham, a third-year university student. Mr. Praj and I hit it off from the aforementioned date and have since shared the pleasure of many conversations.

Consequently, a close friendship has developed. Nearly a year has now elapsed; our friendship remains firm, and is forecast to flourish further in the future, a welcome surprise. Notwithstanding my seniority in age (a matter of a full five years) I hereby grant Mr. Praj Preungtham official permission to append the crude prefix "Ei" to either my first name or nickname, whenever the use of either such is necessary. I swear not to take offense at his addressing me in such a manner. Furthermore, if Mr. Praj does not consider me a close enough friend for us to be on "Ei" terms, I shall terminate the friendship and shall wish upon him a restless death without the possibility of reincarnation. I certify by my honour that the words in this letter reflect my true intentions.

Signed,

Theppitak Rakakart (Ploang)

[Ei Ploang's squiggly signature appeared under his neatly written name]

Back when Ei Ploang was still Khun Ploang to me, his entire body seemed to radiate an aura. He just had to sit there, and it would appear as if a universe revolved around him. It made you wary of approaching him; for fear a meteorite might strike you down. His eyes appeared to house molten volcanoes, or brewing storms, or whirling tsunamis, or high-voltage electricity exploding in a short-circuit, or those damned downpours that dump their loads on you then proceed to dribble for the next couple of hours, or black holes ready to swallow up time, or evil spirits lying in wait to prey on a wandering soul.

I had to wait until he closed his eyes before I had the guts to go over and say hello.

"Are you sleeping?" I asked, gingerly lowering myself onto the same bench.

"Just resting my eyes." Ei Ploang answered promptly and clearly, without bothering to actually open his eyes and examine his questioner.

In those days I regularly woke up early to go jogging in Lumpini Park. School was out, and as my internship hadn't started yet, I wanted to find a productive outlet for my nervous energy. Jogging in the park was a popular past-time, and apparently just as beneficial for your physical health as for your mental well-being. So I thought I'd try the trend myself and give the sportswear stuffed at the bottom of my wardrobe an airing in the light of day.

The first morning I stepped inside Lumpini Park, it isn't strictly accurate to say that I went jogging. Let's just call it a reconnoitre before the actual expedition. When I first arrived, I was stunned by the sheer number of those engaging in exercise, which far exceeded my expectation. I strolled around and, when I got tired, stopped to take in the birds and trees, the dogs and cats and ants, the way animal lovers do. Once I'd had my fill of the various flora and fauna, I resumed walking. That morning, I never even broke into a run.

As I became a frequent visitor to the park, my leg muscles started of their own accord to yearn for stimulation. Soon I was one of those runners, floating along to the beat of hundreds or thousands of human hearts, moving in tandem like ants in a colony. But we weren't worker ants. We didn't run in single file, intent on the survival of the majority. We didn't carry food on our backs to distribute later. We ran for personal reasons, some for fitness, some for vanity, some to reduce stress, and some to ease loneliness.

Then we all went our separate ways.

I'd seen Ei Ploang several times before I decided to stick my nose in and chat him up. Ei Ploang never ran; he never even got up to stretch. He just sat there scanning his surroundings with his mysterious eyes, as if looking for someone he knew. As far as I could tell, no such acquaintance ever presented themselves. Or else, nobody ever dared claim acquaintance with him.

Some days he chose to sit by the pond, staring blankly at the ducks and geese and turtles and fish that surfaced every now and then in search of scraps of food. As far I could tell, none of these ducks, geese, turtles or fish were his especial acquaintance, either. But Ei Ploang always showed up, as if he was sure that one day he would find what he was searching for.

Ei Ploang was, without doubt, a good-looking guy. His eyes were big and round. His reddish-brown skin was smooth in the morning sun. His dark brown hair was razored short on the sides all the way around, sort of like a crew cut. It was plain to see that he didn't come to Lumpini Park to exercise. He usually wore a white shirt and khaki trousers. Some days he was even more smartly dressed, even going so far as to wear a tie.

When Ei Ploang opened his eyes, I was confronted with a pair of huge pupils staring at my face. They remained fixed on it for several seconds, to the point that I was afraid I would fall into their twin black holes and be devoured.

"Oh, it's you. You come jogging here every day."

"You've seen me?" I asked, even though I knew the answer.

"Several times."

"I've noticed you myself. You often sit here, but you never go for a run."

"That's because I don't come here to run." When he finished his sentence, his gaze shifted to a new target. Mine followed his out of curiosity.

His new mark was a chubby woman jouncing along the path. A little girl with braids was trailing close behind her.

"See that auntie? If you look with your bare eyes, just a passing glance, she'd appear to be a good-hearted lady – fond of her niece, makes an effort to get up early so the two of them can spend some time together, instilling healthy habits, etc."

Ei Ploang turned his face toward the sky as if to rest his eyes before he continued talking.

"But in fact, you'd be quite mistaken. She's a mean one, all right. I feel bad for the kid, having to hang around someone so temperamental this early in the morning."

"Do you know them?"

Ei Ploang shook his head and stared into my eyes once more.

"You're a good person. I knew it from the first day I saw you. A little too lazy. A little too inclined to follow trends. You tend to do things half way, you're not as focused as you should be. But, overall, a pretty decent guy."

I remained speechless for a long moment. Not because I was touched by his praise, but simply because I was mystified.

"Look at that middle-aged man."

I snapped myself out of it and, following Ei Ploang's cue, turned to look at the bald man running by. His face suggested one content with the quality of air in the park.

Ei Ploang was tight-lipped, so I tried to guess his mind.

"He looks happy, but he's actually mean like that lady we just saw." This was half statement, half question.

Ei Ploang cracked a smile, the corners of his mouth twitching up.

"It's not always so tricky. Good can show itself in the face, too. You can still find it sometimes. That man's as nice as his face would lead you to believe. He's a lovely guy. Likes to help others. Loves peace."

"You come here every morning expressly for this? To see who's good and who's bad?"

"It's a convenient place for it; all I have to do is sit here, and all kinds of people pass by for me to look at. I don't have to waste my energy traipsing around the streets."

"Some days I don't see you looking at anyone."

"Hey, good and evil aren't only present in humans. Sometimes I practice looking at other things. The difference is, the quantities of good and evil are never equal in humans, while other things have more of a balance. Good and evil don't mean that much when they're in balance. You don't really need to look."

Ei Ploang nudged a pebble with the toe of his shoe, and it rolled forward two or three times. "That pebble has good and evil, too. But it's meaningless to speak of a pebble being either good or evil, because its good and evil are so perfectly balanced as to be inconsequential. It's doing a fine job of functioning as a pebble. If you kick it, it rolls over. But if I kicked you, you wouldn't just roll over."

That morning, Ei Ploang's special ability didn't elicit much admiration from me. Instead, I thought what a weird guy he was; he must have some deep psychological issues. Wanting to sneak away from the bench, I pretended that I had to continue running. Ei Ploang responded with a smile and a nod. Before I was too far off, he tossed out a casual remark. "Don't fear the good in yourself."

I may have thought he was mad, but his ideas stuck in my head for the whole rest of the day. When I got home, I stood in front of the mirror and stared at myself for almost half an hour, to the point that I lost track of who was doing the staring. In the end, I thought it more likely that my reflection was looking at me.

Come to think of it, it's laughable that I gave Ei Ploang any credence. In this day and age, we're developed enough to understand that being a good or bad person doesn't have meaning anymore. Even if you're the most heinous person in history, there'll be others who are cut from the same heinous cloth, allies who'll go along with your beliefs and actions. In the eyes of people of the same ilk, good can still appear within evil. What's the point of getting hung up about having to cede the moral high ground when there's plenty of people to pal around with down below? Let those on the high ground gasp in the thin air. Let them get struck by lightning. What's so great about that? Being close to the ground is so much safer.

Evil is usually accompanied by ingenuity and resourcefulness in saving yourself, a talent for constantly getting out of scrapes and for pulling the wool over people's eyes. A bad person can make himself appear good, but a good person will never truly understand evil. Everybody knows that human society can't maintain its structures on good alone. It's plain to see that evil is the key component in governing the world. If everyone were good, there would be no politicians, and if this world were free of politicians, human society would lack organisation, regulation, and ammunition, all crucial weapons for wiping out a mess in order to start over, for example, by pushing a button to erase all the previous wrongs and start wrongdoing all over again. Evil is the mother of opportunity. Good would never be that creative. Evil is art and entertainment; good is bland and boring.

Why should I care if I'm going to heaven or hell? Both places are founded upon beliefs that are fading over time. Evil teaches people to stop being hung up on superstitions. It teaches us to learn to live life fully here on this earth. Even if you're condemned to boil in hell's cauldron or drag your naked body up the adulterers' thorny tree, you'd be sharing in those activities with your fellow sinners. It's no different from going on summer camp. Everyone would rather meet the Guardian of Hell than God, because the Guardian of Hell is humanity's true teacher, covertly indoctrinating us from the cradle. He stands close by us when we want, when we hurt, when we ache, when we love, when we lust, when we hate, when we obsess, when we're hungry, when we're greedy, when we're angry, when we're vengeful.

God only watches from afar. He never lends a helping hand.

So why did Ei Ploang's words strike such a chord with me?

Why should I be proud of being a good person in his eyes?

I've been searching for the answer ever since.

Maybe good has a charm that evil doesn't.

Because good isn't something that I'm acquainted with.

After that, whenever I saw Ei Ploang sitting there judging people with nothing but his eyes, I couldn't stop myself. I had to sit down and scan people along with him, and eventually I started going to Lumpini Park in my normal street clothes, expressly to sit and look at people with him. I'd completely forgotten about jogging.

Ei Ploang never taught me how to judge people, and I never pressed him to.

Once other business entered into my life, I didn't go and sit with him as regularly as before. I went only on some Saturdays or Sundays when I had the time.

It was on one such Saturday morning that Ei Ploang gave me the slip of paper permitting me to call him "Ei." I'd deliberately got up early that day, to go to Lumpini Park and see him. I'd never made plans to meet up with him anywhere else or at any other time. I didn't even have his phone number, this friend of mine. He wasn't a part of my everyday life. One reason for this was that I feared his judging those close to me. I didn't want to hear that my mother was evil, my father was bad, or my friend was a low-down good-for-nothing. Even if I had decided for myself that everybody in my circle was a good person, I had to admit that I didn't have Ei Ploang's unique gift. He might know better and see more deeply. So, naturally, I was worried.

But Ei Ploang himself never asked about my life outside of the park. He said hi when he saw me. He said bye when I left. That was it.

Ei Ploang never got up from the bench before I did. He never took leave of me first. I've never once seen him set foot beyond the bounds of Lumpini Park. Perhaps he lives right in there. I've never asked him about his home. Each morning, we were hard pressed as it was to keep up with the stream of people jogging or walking by. There wasn't much time left to quiz each other on personal matters.

Even though Ei Ploang gave me permission to call him "Ei," I didn't have many occasions to exercise my special right. When we were face to face, there was no need for me to call him by name. When I was with other people, I rarely brought him up, because no one else knew him. Everyone I mentioned him to all thought he was my imaginary friend. No one paid much attention to his name. When I tell people at home that I was off to Lumpini Park to see Ei Ploang, they'd just respond with an ah-ha or an okay, or they'd ask me to pick up some food at the park. Nobody bothered to find out who Ei Ploang was.

After I'd finished reading Ei Ploang's permission slip, right down to his signature, I sat down to study people with him as usual. He pointed out this one and that one for me to look at, in the usual way he had. Good here, evil there, all mingled together.

There were, of course, more bad people than good. In a group of a hundred, Ei Ploang saw fewer than twenty good ones.

"Hey, how the hell do you know I'm a good guy?" I finally asked him the question I'd been putting off for ages, afraid that he wouldn't answer. I purposely added "the hell" as a nod to his new "Ei" status.

Ei Ploang didn't smile as I'd expected he would. Nor did he turn to look at me, either.

"I thought you'd have asked a long time ago," he said softly.

"I didn't have the goddamned courage before. I was afraid you wouldn't tell me." I intentionally threw in the "goddamned" to match the "Ei" and the "hell" I'd just used.

Ei Ploang let out a huge sigh. *Huuuh.*

"Should I tell him?" Ei Ploang asked himself out loud.

I watched joggers and walkers of all ages pass in front of us, from our left and from our right, heading in opposite directions. In just a few seconds, there were more than I could count on two hands.

"You don't have to tell me," I said to Ei Ploang without turning to look at him.

I put his permission slip into my shirt pocket.

Behind the piece of paper was the fabric of my shirt. Behind the fibres of the cloth was skin. Underneath the skin was a web of interconnected vessels. Within those little vessels was the liquid being pumped to sustain the body.

Only a feeling tells you that it's a manifestation of being.

My eyes couldn't see to that level of detail.

I turned to look at my friend.

Ei Ploang was resting his eyes.

A SCHOOLGIRL'S DIARY

1. LITTLE MISS TONG-JAI IN OTHER PEOPLE'S EYES; LITTLE MISS TONG-JAI IN HER OWN EYES

Tong-Jai wants to have a heart attack.

Because she's heard that it's the most sudden and least painful way to die.

Tong-Jai is nine years old.

Tong-Jai is in Fourth Grade, Section Three, whose form teacher is Ms. Bacon.

Tong-Jai's school has a gym teacher also named Bacon, but he is a man. The students refer to the female teacher as Ms. Bacon and the male teacher as Mr. Bacon, so there's no confusion. The school has another female teacher named Bacon, but the other Ms. Bacon is a sixth-grade teacher and has a fuller figure, so the students call Tong-Jai's form teacher Skinny Ms. Bacon and the sixth-grade teacher Fat Ms. Bacon.

Some call them Ms. Bacon Four and Ms. Bacon Six, but Tong-Jai is not keen on those tags.

Tong-Jai is not skilled at mathematics.

She doesn't understand one plus one.

Ms. Karmen Rider is the fourth-grade math teacher. (The school has only one teacher named Rider, so there's no need to add a qualifier to her name. Even so, Tong-Jai sometimes hears upper elementary pupils call her Ms. Rider X, which confounds Tong-Jai a great deal. Little Mr. Toey, Tong-Jai's classmate in form 4/3, once explained his theory to Tong-Jai: the reason the upper elementary kids call Ms. Rider Ms. Rider X is because she's a tough homework grader, who makes especially frequent use of the cross mark, X. Although Toey's theory has enough evidence to be credible, Tong-Jai isn't quite convinced. Her instincts tell her that the reason the older kids call the teacher Ms. Rider X has something to do with the X-rated size of her chest, which is unusually well-endowed.)

Ms. Rider once threw a piece of chalk at Tong-Jai, because of Tong-Jai's failure to understand one plus one.

Tong-Jai's one plus one equals either one or three.

Why does one plus one equal one or three, Tong-Jai? Ms. Rider was baffled.

Because I'm not sure which answer is more correct.

They're both wrong. Class, can you please tell Tong-Jai the right answer, loud and clear? What's one plus one?

One! Plus! One! Equals! Two!, the students in form 4/3 shouted.

Correct. Very good. Did you hear that, Tong-Jai? Your classmates all know that one plus one is two. Two it is. Two, not one or three. Didn't you already learn this in kindergarten?

How does one plus one make two? Wait. If you have one, where does the other one come from? And why do they put themselves together? Just that is a knotty issue in itself. Suppose Dad is one, plus another one, Mom. That equals three, obviously, because when those two joined together, I was born, making three. Plus, suppose Mom and Dad's combination doesn't end here. If later on I have a little sibling, that makes four. Then if my little sibling gets a little sibling, that makes five. Suppose one is a tiger and another one is a rabbit. If you put them together, the tiger would eat the rabbit, so there's only one left. Suppose one is mercury, and you add more mercury

– mercury plus mercury makes one big chunk of mercury – that turns out to be one again.

Tong-Jai doesn't understand the number two.

Where does two come from?

Ms. Rider didn't understand Tong-Jai. Ms. Rider couldn't take it anymore. She grabbed a piece of chalk from the blackboard and threw it at the girl, hitting her on the left cheek, just hard enough for it to cause a slight itch.

Tong-Jai rubbed her cheek a little, but only because of the itch.

No piece of chalk had struck Ms. Rider, but of the two of them, she looked the more in pain. Tears streamed down the apples of her cheeks.

Ms. Rider approached Tong-Jai and crouched down to pick up the piece of chalk from the floor.

I'm sorry, Tong-Jai. Please be a good girl. Believe me, one plus one is two.

Tong-Jai stood still with her top and bottom lips sealed into one single, indivisible whole.

She nodded just a fraction, in deference to an adult's tears.

Suppose a teardrop falls and combines with another teardrop, that makes one big teardrop...

Tong-Jai summarised in her head:

One plus one equals one sixty percent of the time. One plus one equals three or more forty percent of the time.

Since that day, whenever an adult asked Tong-Jai what one plus one makes, she would answer two, unless the asker was a child or an elderly person, in which case she would say, greater or less than two.

Tong-Jai concluded that answering in accordance with the opinion of the majority was a requisite for getting by in life.

But answering in accordance to one's own beliefs was a requisite for sleeping soundly at night.

Tong-Jai further concluded that between the one who throws the projectile and the one who gets struck by it, the former feels the greater pain.

Skinny Ms. Bacon thinks that Tong-Jai will probably grow up to be a sharp-tongued politician, because she has observed during school debates that Tong-Jai has a knack for tirelessly defending the arguments she comes up with. Even though Tong-Jai's points often had nothing to do with the topic assigned, even though at times they clearly contradicted her own team's position, Tong-Jai would argue and argue and argue her point until the last second. And in the end Tong-Jai would always lose, because she would confound the judges.

Even so, Skinny Ms. Bacon is convinced that her pupil will grow up to be a star orator, one whose role in shaping the wisdom of the nation will be influential, whether large or small. But more likely large than small, if she had to guess.

Tong-Jai wants to grow up to be a female shot-put athlete.

Sometimes Tong-Jai wants to grow up to be a stamp affixer at the post office.

If her dreams come true and she gets to be a post-office worker, Tong-Jai would love to lick the customers' stamps for them, feeling that if her saliva gets to travel to faraway places, sometimes even overseas, it's like a part of her is travelling too. It would make her deliriously happy. The job sounds amazing, and challenging.

The reason Tong-Jai wants to be a shot-put athlete is because she wants to hold an object with a lot of weight in her hands and then hurl it far, far away. The reason she wants to be a female shot-put athlete is because she's female.

Tong-Jai's father wants her to be a dentist like him.

Tong-Jai's mother wants her daughter to be a dentist like her husband.

Tong-Jai's favorite subject is LES. LES stands for Life Experience Studies.

Tong-Jai prefers to take in life from reading Life Experience Studies books than from drinking milk.

In the morning, if Tong-Jai's mother asks her:

Have you drunk your milk, Tong-Jai?

Tong-Jai will answer:

There's no need. I have LES today.

Tong-Jai's closest friend at school is Pui.

The boys like to call her POO-ey and then laugh themselves into stitches.

Tong-Jai doesn't understand why it's so funny.

Tong-Jai and Pui always pair up to eat lunch. Pui's grandmother is a great cook, but Tong-Jai's favorites are the sweets that Pui brings with her every day, which are usually chocolates.

Tong-Jai doesn't get to eat chocolate much because her father's a dentist. Dentists don't like chocolate. But Tong-Jai likes chocolate a lot.

Pui knows Tong-Jai likes chocolate, so she always brings some extra to share with her friend. Sometimes Tong-Jai and Pui top their rice with chocolate, instead of with stir fry or curry.

Once, Skinny Ms. Bacon witnessed this and went over to lecture the girls on their conduct.

You shouldn't eat rice with chocolate, you know. It's not nutritious. Give me the chocolate. I'll hold on to it until school gets out, and then I'll give it back.

Now eat your rice with the dishes that your families prepared for you. I want to see you eat it all up.

Tong-Jai burst into tears.

Pui looked at her with pity. Pui considers her friend the type that's committed to what she loves. Naturally, she can't bear it when she's forced to part with something she holds dear.

After school that day, Skinny Ms. Bacon didn't return the chocolate to Tong-Jai and Pui as promised. They never saw the chocolate again.

Tong-Jai announced to Pui that in future, if anyone at school promised to do something after school, she would first negotiate for it to be done a little before the end of the school day, because once school was out, her student status was temporarily suspended and she had no power to demand anything.

The following day, Tong-Jai tried to sneak a peek at Skinny Ms. Bacon's gums, to see if she could detect any dark brown traces.

Tong-Jai had made up her mind that, if she saw any, she would call the police.

2. "MY HOUSE," A COMPOSITION BY LITTLE MISS TONG-JAI

My house has two floors. The upper floor is eleven steps higher than the lower one. Sometimes I walk upstairs. Sometimes my father carries me up. It depends on whether I've fallen asleep watching TV that night. If I don't, I walk myself up. If I do, then my father carries me up. Some nights my father tries to wake me to walk myself up, but I don't wake up easily, or if I do wake up, I'm too groggy and my father has to carry me up anyway.

My house is a cement house. My mother said my house used to be made of wood but then my father tore it down and rebuilt it using cement. I can't confirm that, though, because that was before I was born. My house is white. The roof is made of yellow tiles. Sometimes when it rains hard, rainwater leaks into the house. My mother said our roof had a leak, but I've never seen where it is because I've never been on the roof. I once asked my father if I could go up and see where the hole was. My father said I had to wait until I got bigger before he would take me up. I'm afraid that before that happens, the hole will have grown so large that the rain floods our house. If I drown, I won't get to see the hole on the roof.

My father said, don't worry, he'd buy a boat to be prepared – no matter what happens, I won't die from drowning.

My house has four human inhabitants and one dog. My dog is named Spot because he has black dots all over his body, as if someone drew spots on him. My mother said he was born that way. But I think my father might have dribbled black ink on him when he was still little, because my father once spilled black ink on the living room rug, and it left a blotch exactly like the dots on Spot's body, and it also didn't wash off. I've asked my father if he dripped ink on Spot. He repeatedly denied it. He refuses to confess.

The four people in my house are me, my father, my mother and Pi Nid. Pi Nid is my nanny, but when I'm not home she has plenty of other things to do, like sweeping, mopping, doing laundry, ironing, washing the dishes, and cooking. Sometimes Pi Nid gets scolded by my parents. Sometimes the scolding makes her cry, and then she comes to complain to me that my parents are mean. I myself don't understand why Pi Nid lives at my house if she thinks that my parents are mean. I asked Pi Nid why she doesn't run away if she doesn't like my mother and father. She said she can't because she has to work and earn money to support her mother back home in the provinces.

I don't know what Pi Nid's house is like because I've never been there, but my house has two floors.

My house was robbed once. I think the robber slipped in through the hole in the roof. My father said the robber pried the window open to break in, but if there's already a hole in the roof, why would you waste your time and energy with the window? Mr. or Ms. Robber (I don't know if the robber was male or female) took four things: a TV, my father's big stereo, a VCR and a vacuum cleaner – all big, heavy things, which might explain why he or she had to crank the window open; to carry the big items out more conveniently. In that case, it's possible that the robber slipped in through the hole in the roof and then escaped through the window afterward. See, if the robber had chosen to take only small objects, he or she probably could have slipped back out through the hole in the roof and wouldn't have had to spend so much effort wrestling with the window.

After my house got robbed, I didn't have a TV to watch for days, almost a whole week. So all that week I was able to walk myself up the stairs to go to bed, because I went to sleep earlier than normal. My parents were irritated that they couldn't listen to music on the stereo, couldn't catch any series on TV and couldn't rent any videos. I felt like that week my house had more dust than before because we didn't have a vacuum, but no one seemed to miss the vacuum much. Pi Nid even seemed happy that the robber stole the vacuum cleaner. Luckily, Spot didn't get stolen, too. I would miss him the most if he'd been carried off. But as far as I know, robbers tend not to steal living things.

My house faces northwest. I've never measured it myself, but my father once said, "Did you know, Tong-Jai, that our house faces northwest?" I didn't know. Now that I know, I want to know northwhat I face. My father said people keep changing the direction they face because animals are living things, which don't stay still. But I think it wouldn't be too bad if we had devices we could attach to ourselves to tell us northwhat we were facing at any given time. My father said a device like that already exists. It's called a compass, and it has a magnetic needle. If I held a compass all the time, I would always know which direction I was facing. I asked my father to buy me a compass. He said he would get me one as a present for my birthday, which is still a while away. My father often says he'll buy me something for my birthday. I'm probably going to get a lot of presents for my birthday this year. But right now, what I want most is a compass. Once I get one, I'll have to be very careful, because if not I might prick my finger with the magnetic needle, which seems like it would hurt more than getting pricked by a regular needle.

Now that I think about it, I kind of understand why the robber didn't steal Spot (even though he's very cute). It's probably because Spot is a living thing and doesn't stay put. He keeps changing directions, and that would cause the robber constant annoyance and confusion over north which he was facing. Even I get annoyed that I have to wait until my birthday to find out which way I'm facing.

My house is down a side street, but it's not very far down. It's only about a five-minute walk from the top of the street. If you're tired, it might take a little more than five minutes, probably about seven and half minutes, which is not the house's fault because my house can't move. It just sits there like that. Whether it takes a little or a lot of time to get from the top of the street to the house depends on the walker. If you ride down in a car, it's even a few minutes faster than walking. But if the car breaks down or bumps into another car first, you might never reach my house. Therefore, if you're going to come in a car, you should be sure to fasten the seat belt properly. If you ride on the back of a motorbike, don't forget to put on a helmet.

I think my house is beautiful. But others might look at it and see an ordinary house with nothing special, which might be because others don't yet know northwhat my house faces.

MISS SPACE

When, in early elementary school, I had just started learning to write, the teacher taught us to put our index fingers between sentences to ensure neat, even spaces throughout the composition.

Years later, after I'd mastered writing (or at least scrawling), the index-finger system was ignored and eventually abandoned. The spaces between sentences were liberated from their regulator and put in charge of their own arrangement. An up-to-me anarchy prevailed. Without checks and bounds, the letters became brash – they got loose, lax and liquidy, lumped together or leaning forwards and backwards in a carefree and shameless manner.

Even so, the size of my spaces could still be described as normal. It didn't strike the eye as odd, unlike those produced by the following person:

Miss Wondee.

She was in her early twenties. Her birth fell on a hot, sunny noon. The doctor who performed the delivery was in a bad mood that day. He had diarrhea and a backache, and his recurrent migraine was also acting up. Yet he upheld his duty, seamlessly managing to pull out the head of a bright pink, grumpy-faced baby girl. When the umbilical cord linking mother and child was snipped, one life became two.

The baby girl screamed as if she regretted being born. Her mother gathered her strength and turned to look, with concerned tenderness, at the infant who had inhabited her body for several months:

This is the first minute of life in the outside world? How miraculous and how pitiful at the same time. Baby, don't cry. This is all there is to life: live for a while, eat, sleep, learn from books made up of other people's ideas, meet all kinds of folks, some you'll love, some you'll hate. When you meet the one you hate least, you can be together, help each other along as you eat and sleep and earn baht to exchange for possessions. If you want a lot of possessions, you'll have to earn a lot of baht. If you're lucky (or unlucky), you'll live to be old. Sometimes you're tired, sometimes bored, sometimes sad, sometimes happy – that's all life is. You won't have to wait too long before you die.

I first met Miss Wondee on the bus. We were sitting next to each other, and she was bent over scribbling something. She had a notebook with yellow paper on her lap and a 2B pencil in her right hand. My nose and the ease with which it tended towards its adjective made me sneak a look at what she was writing, to see whether it was a worthy object of my attention.

It was then that I noticed the extraordinary size of Miss Wondee's spaces. Four twenty-five pm, to be exact. The air-conditioned (the condition of the air went from good to bad) bus was turning right at the intersection. The driver had twangy upcountry music playing faintly on the radio. The lyrics recounted the classic story about a farmer coming to the big city to look for his girlfriend, who had left the provinces to sell herself under the neon lights.

I remember all this in such detail because of the size of Miss Wondee's spaces. They catalysed my consciousness as though it had been struck by lightning, and I briefly became abnormally perceptive, able to absorb information about my environment instantaneously and effortlessly. Thank god I stopped just short of Nirvana.

Wondee was writing a diary entry: what she did, whom she saw, who called, when she went to bed. It was your average entry, and my staring didn't manage to pinpoint minor details. What was more interesting than the letters that lined up to create meaning were the areas between each thought: they were about as long as the sentences themselves. It was as if they were there to provide breathing room, so that each letter could inhale and exhale comfortably.

"Excuse me," I said softly, fearing that I'd break her concentration.

She didn't hear me, or pretended not to. Or she heard me but was afraid to talk to a male stranger on the bus. Or she heard me and didn't want to be bothered. Or she half heard me. (She might have been prevented from hearing both words clearly by the noise from the bus engine, which cycled between loud and soft, so perhaps she was unsure whether I was talking to her or whether I was a crazy person talking to myself.)

"Excuse me. Please forgive my indiscretion, but my meddlesome eyes happened to notice your writing. Please don't think that I was snooping – not at all! You could've been writing the most intimate things about yourself, but I didn't read any of it, and I wouldn't dare to. And if I accidentally read some, I'll gladly erase that bit of my memory in the next few seconds. Trust me, I don't mean to pry into your personal business, but the reason I'm chatting you up like this is, I noticed how bizarrely you arrange your writing. I can't hold back my curiosity. Can I ask you a question? I hope you don't mind."

After such a lengthy spiel, she'd have to turn around and look at me, even if she hadn't been able to catch what I was saying. Her irises, black as tamarind seeds, didn't flicker. The outer corners of her eyes angled down toward her cheek bones, like the downward-curving eyes of a laughing Buddha, but one that wasn't laughing or smiling. She stared at my face before dragging out the words: *What did you say?*

"It's like this," I turned toward her about thirty degrees, started gesturing with my hands, making the same preparations for a serious conversation as I'd witnessed from academics on television.

"Your spacing has left a big impression on me." She looked down at the notebook on her lap.

"I don't know if you're conscious of it, but the way you space is extraordinary. When, in early elementary school, I had just started learning to write, the teacher taught us to put our index fingers between sentences to ensure neat, even spaces throughout the composition. Years later, after I'd mastered writing (or at least scrawling), the index-finger system was ignored and eventually abandoned. The spaces between sentences have been liberated from their regulator and put in charge of their own arrangement. An up-to-me anarchy prevails. Without checks and bounds, the letters have become brash – they've got loose, lax and liquidy, and now lump together or lean forwards and backwards in a carefree and shameless manner.

"Even so, the size of my spaces can still be described as normal. It doesn't strike the eye as odd. But look at yours. Your spacing is abnormally large. One might say that you give as much weight to the spaces as the letters in your sentences. Or maybe even more. When I look at the page you have there, the first thing I see are the spaces, not the letters. So, I wanted to ask: is that intentional, or is it a deranged childhood habit you can't break? For me, I see a whole range of potential philosophical takes on it. For example, perhaps you're suggesting that meaning and blankness have equal importance. Or you're conveying something about intervals in the thought process and how they should contain pauses to leave room for further possibilities to develop. Or your spaces are comparable to shadows of memory, left as a hint that memory is not a substitute for the truth, not a record of history, but rather a shadow, a residual feeling left over from the past.

"Am I getting warm with my analysis? I'd be grateful if you'd be so kind as to reveal the origins of your idiosyncratic manner of spacing."

She sat there frozen for a moment. Her right hand was tightly clutching the 2B pencil. Her other hand was spread over the yellow page of her notebook. Maybe she was trying to conceal the idiosyncrasy between her sentences, out of embarrassment (or fear). The paper beneath her palm started to shrivel as the sweat seeped out through her pores.

A moment later, her lips began to part.

"I'm sorry. My name's Wondee. I've got to go – you made me miss my stop several minutes ago. If I don't get off at the next stop, I'll have to walk much further than I want to. I'm wearing new shoes – I can't walk too much in them or I'll get blisters. So please excuse me, but I have to get off. Although I don't quite understand what you were saying, I'm happy to talk to you, but it'd have to be another day. I'll write my number down for you."

Wondee looked down. Her pencil began to move. Then, with the hand that was holding the pencil, she tore off a corner from a page of her notebook and handed it to me.

Seven digits were written on the piece of paper in this manner:

6 3 4 8 6 5 4

Even for numbers, she made (no) room for exception.

The word "space" seems an architectural word. When it was adapted for use in orthography, it must have become abstracted and linked to the art of the optical – leaving blank spaces in a way that's easy on the eyes and comfortable to read. If you were to call them "blanks," the connotation would be undesirably negative. These areas may not hold anything, but they're not empty – they clearly have their own special function.

Even though the origin of the word "space" could be considered more or less acceptable, I wasn't satisfied with it. For me, it's too strong a word, and lacks a creative meaning. (The word "space" makes me feel like my letters could vanish into thin air at any moment. This feeling presents a major obstacle to writing.)

When I got home that day, the day I met the spacer named Wondee, I tried while sitting down, while lying down, while showering, while brushing my teeth, to come up with a more suitable word.

Eventually, I landed on the term "waiting period".

Here, "waiting" means waiting for the next thought. Waiting for the mood. Waiting remains a mere act of hope – what you're waiting for may never come. The word is broad and inconclusive. After I resolved to coin a new term, Miss Wondee's spaces became even more interesting.

At the office the next day, as I was staring into space while I waited for my lunch break (I work for an insurance company. I have to volunteer the fact that I do it only to support myself. In actuality, I have thoughts that are deeper and more complicated than most salarymen do. Please don't judge me by my vocation. I'd suggest using other indicators, for example: I don't eat meat; I don't carry a wallet; I don't smoke; I don't support spending people's tax on weapons of mass destruction; I'd definitely protest against a war wherever and whenever.), I pulled a scrap of yellow paper out of my trouser pocket and dialed Miss Wondee's seven digits on my phone.

No one answered. *Please leave a message.*

I didn't leave a message. How am I supposed to leave one, just like that?

Then it occurred to me that the seven digits were probably her home phone number, and she was unlikely to be in during office or school hours. I ought to wait and try her again closer to sundown.

As it turned out, I didn't have to wait until I got home. By the powers that be, Miss Wondee and I took the same bus again. Although space was tight on the bus this time, meaning we had to chat while standing and hanging on to the rail, the overall atmosphere was not very different from the previous day. The tune playing softly on the radio was different, but it was still about a country girl who'd come to the city only to shed tears and lose heart working the bathtub at a massage parlour. You can't help but be moved when you listen to that song. You want to be the hero who marches in and liberates these girls from the depths of hell. It's like freeing living things from a zoo.

Miss Wondee was rather surprised to see me again. But this time she smiled. Her expression and the downward curvature of her eyes made her the spitting image of a laughing Buddha, albeit a female one.

"It must be tricky to write in your diary when you have to hold on to the rail like this."

She laughed, just enough to be polite.

"So, will you tell me why you space so strangely?"

"It's quite a waste of paper."

"But that's not the point." My academic side reared its head once more.

"Whether or not it's a waste of paper is an issue of conflict between capitalism and the environment. I don't care about that. That's a persistent issue that's never going to disappear as long as the exchange system continues to hold sway among societies. What I'm interested in is the influence of the system of collective psychology on the structure of individ-ual psychology, namely, a person's psyche, which is shaped by external forces. For example, let's say I'm A, and I obsessively rub my palms together when I'm not paying attention. When you investigate the cause of this compulsion, you discover that I was an active child, that I used to run into things and break all kinds of stuff on a daily basis. My behavior was judged by external forces, a.k.a. society, to be annoying and exasperating: What an unmindful little monkey! The group of external people called society ('external' here meaning external to my conscious mind) – or one could call them the adults at home – therefore punished me by slapping my hands – pap! pap! – until they were red and swollen as a pair of boxing gloves. With such punishment inflicted on a regular basis, the hand-rubbing habit automatically sunk into the structure of my psyche. Out of habit, the former child continues to rub his palms into adulthood, and may keep doing so until his life is over."

The bus jerked. Every part of my body above the belt leaned forward, almost bumping into every part of Miss Wondee's body above the skirt. Alas, the bus pulled itself together in time, so the collision between two warm-blooded animals didn't happen. But at least the part of me called the nose got close enough to sniff Miss Wondee's jet-black hair. My candid review: it smelled nice.

"Now, back to your spacing. I'm dying to know the history of your behavior, your way of forming spaces – which I shall henceforth call 'waiting periods.' Did something happen to you when you were a child? Or are you intentionally projecting a certain image of yourself? Are you acting odd to attract attention?"

Miss Wondee blinked helplessly at me as the bus decelerated.

"I missed my stop again. Excuse me."

Then she wedged her way through the crowd, liberating herself from the oppression of the public transportation machinery and leaving me standing there with my tongue as dry as the Sahara.

"Ticket check, please."

A small-framed woman in a blue uniform, who had a gift for wriggling smoothly through the push and shove, looked up at me with pity.

I didn't have the nerve to call Miss Wondee again, but I must admit that I learned the seven digits of her phone number by heart.

Sometimes, when things were slow at work and I was just sitting at my desk, I would stare at the buttons on my phone and dial Miss Wondee's number in my head. It was such pathetic behavior, probably with complex origins dating back to my early infancy. I hadn't found time to analyse it yet. All my free time was devoted to this funny feeling that distracted me.

Was I being brainwashed? Was Miss Wondee's spacing an ingenious mechanism for staging a psychological coup? Or were her spaces really waiting periods? I myself was certainly in a fever of anticipation!

—

About three weeks – the individual units of which were two million four hundred fourteen thousand and four hundred seconds – later, which to me was a rather long time, the wind from the bus's air conditioner blew Miss Wondee my way again. I saw her even before I placed my left foot up onto the bus. She was sitting by the window, looking down. Her hair, as shiny as if she'd put shoe polish on it, looked almost unrecognizably long. Time tends to make all kinds of things expand. If you leave them alone, things can stretch, lengthen, heighten, widen, swell and puff up.

I tried to muffle the excited boom of my heartbeat, but the pulse in my feet didn't cooperate. As soon as I boarded the bus, I made a beeline for the space by the window. A glum-looking middle-aged woman was sitting next to Miss Wondee, so I had to perform some minor gymnastics, getting up on my tiptoes and leaning over the woman's head, to make myself conspicuous. But Miss Wondee still didn't notice me. She was writing in her yellow-paper diary with the concentration of a meditating hermit. The waiting periods on the page were still as odd and interesting as when they first caught my eye.

Surprisingly, the glum-looking woman didn't pay the slightest attention to Miss Wondee's spacing. What can you do? Some people, even when a miracle appears right in front of their nose, remain perfectly oblivious. What a shame.

I craned my neck awkwardly for several seconds without any reaction before I took the liberty of stretching my left hand out to tap Miss Wondee on the shoulder. I almost hit Glum Face on the temple, but curved away just in time. Miss Wondee looked up from the yellow paper, and the female laughing Buddha was back.

"Hi. Writing in your diary again? At a quick glance, from where I'm standing, your waiting periods are still adept at keeping their special distance."

The glum-faced woman probably couldn't take it anymore, or maybe the word "period" had offended her female sensibilities. In any case, she got up and surrendered her seat to me, despite the fact that I was neither a pregnant woman, a child, an elderly or disabled person, a monk or a novice.

"I've spent the three weeks since I last saw you constructively. I've been analysing it in my head.

"And referring to the textbooks I had on hand. Even Sigmund Freud wasn't much help. Carl Jung was none at all. But don't worry, I used my own judgment and common sense to analyse this meticulously. I believe I've come to some pretty decent preliminary conclusions regarding your special behavior. First, let me say, your manner of spacing must surely relate to your family fundamentals. Even when they're not the dominant cause, fundamentals inevitably affect secondary factors, which may be more visible.

"I venture to say that you have a lot of siblings, all born rather far apart. The sibling relations, therefore, developed abnormally. Even worse, I speculate that either your mother or father passed away when you were still quite young. But as I hinted earlier, these things may not be the main determinant. That, I believe, can be traced to your respiratory system. This is a bold speculation on my part given that it has to do with your anatomy, which I have no knowledge of. But let me guess first – please don't reveal whether I'm right or wrong until afterwards. My guess is that your circulation system is peculiar: your heart doesn't keep the same beat as normal people's, and that makes your inhalation and exhalation peculiar, too. The frequency with which you expel carbon dioxide and draw in oxygen probably forms a graph with peaks and troughs that resemble a series of elongated hills. This gives you more distance for reflection, *ie*, space for thought, than the average person – about ten seconds' worth. Hence the spaces in your writing, which leave room for reflection."

Miss Wondee appeared to be listening more intently than on the previous occasions, but when I reached that point in my discussion, she shifted, seemingly to get up from her seat.

"We're almost at my stop. I'm sorry."

I leaned aside to let her pass.

Before she slipped out of my radius, I couldn't suppress a final point of interrogation.

"Wondee, are you wearing perfume today?"

Miss Wondee turned back and smiled. The bus was slowing down. Passengers were flocking to the doors.

"See you."

And then she left.

I sat still for another seven waiting periods.

And then I got off.

—

NB: The last sentence is not a conclusion. Rather, it is a waiting period that doesn't yet have a thought to succeed it.

— With Miss Wondee's seal of approval.

SOMETHING IN THE AIR

A cluster of dusky gray clumps hung in the sky above the capital, converging there from all points of the compass. This confluence of water vapour created a state of swollen saturation, a stifling swelter and a rumbling roar. Lightning ripped through the curtain of wind, forking like tree roots, threatening to transform night into day. The sky alternated between light bright enough to expose every nook and cranny of human civilisation, and darkness dredged up from primitive dungeons.

The wind was so strong that the first batch of drops wrung from the clouds couldn't steer a straight path, sending its front guard swerving and skimming the target.

Those that reached the finish line scattered down over satellite dishes, mounted on top of high-rise buildings.

One of the remaining battalions of rain poured down on the roof deck of a four-story townhouse.

The open-air space was walled in with the same streaked and stained white cement from which the entire structure had been constructed. A young man stood there, his legs wide apart. Soaking wet clothes clung to his skin. He wore only an orange T-shirt, black underpants, and nothing on his feet.

Five minutes earlier, while this man was taking in the boom-bang, rumble-tumble, and drip-drop noise coming from outside, and delighting in the moaning and groaning, tossing and turning, nestling and nuzzling action indoors with a smooth-skinned young lady, a curious clash suddenly came from above. His libido interrupted, the man exclaimed in his head: *Shit! Has a plane crashed into my house? A new world war wouldn't make such a din.*

But what materialised before him was not the remnants of an airborne vehicle. Rather, they were two giant red English letters that, before the rain had begun to douse the city, had spelled part of a camera brand name on a thick metal sign on the roof of the building next door. Now they were piled on top of each other in the middle of the rain, on the roof deck of the man who did not wish to disclose his name.

One of the letters was an O; the other was an N. The N was sitting on top of the O.

The man struggled to see through the sheet of rain. When the flash in the sky revealed that one of the letters was an O, his mouth formed a similar ring.

Shortly thereafter, the woman who had been lying spread-eagled, soaked in sweat, in the bedroom on the second floor, emerged at the top of the staircase. She was wearing a white T-shirt and dark blue shorts. Her feet, along with several other bits under the fabric of these items, were naked.

"What happened here?" she said in a high-pitched tone. "There appears to be two large-scale foreign objects piled on top of each other."

The man was still stunned by what had transpired. "Indeed. My theory is that these two English letters received such a blow from the storm that they fell off the metal support and flew down to the spot that you see before you. The crash sounded as if a giant fell off a chair, and that's what startled us in the heat of our domestic activities a moment ago."

The woman nodded, in part to communicate her comprehension and in part to shake a drop of water loose from the tip of her chin. She folded her arms. Every inch of her, from the ends of her hair to the tips of her toenails, was shivering. She tried to shelter under the eaves that jutted out from the doorway leading to the stairs; her white T-shirt was getting splattered nevertheless. Even in the dark, the flesh-coloured mounds of her chest were noticeably protruding. Her dark hair, jet-black in the night, made the radiant skin on her round face glow like the moon.

The light in the sky electrified once more.

Through her wet lips, the woman produced the following: "We were frightened to no small extent, but now that you've done an inspection and determined the sequence of events, you should be satisfied. Why stand exposed to heaven's mood this way? It behooves us to hurry back into the house lest we disturb our bodies' respiratory and immune systems. Have you forgotten that there's a certain business waiting to be resumed? The pores on a human body do not take at all kindly to temperatures such as these."

The young man averted his eyes from the giant letters to consider his female companion through the blanket of rain.

"True. Normally, moments like these are not con-ducive for a visit to the roof deck, but today is a rather special day. Out of nowhere, two large red letters, an N and an O, came crashing down and caused us to act in a way we never would had said incident not occurred – namely, to stand on the roof deck in the middle of a rainstorm, notwithstanding the light and the sound coming from the sky, and during such dark hours. The cold, soggy sensation is passing; the beat of the heart is quickening; the pores are adjusting to the weather. It would be a real shame if we turned our backs on the out-of-bounds experience on this occasion. Why not enjoy each other right here on this roof deck, right under this pounding deluge of water, right next to these two red letters, right at this very moment?"

The woman wore a stupefied expression but was listening closely. She had yet to budge from her spot beneath the eaves. Her shirt was becoming skin-colored, and her dark blue shorts clung to her thighs and the bits between her legs.

The sky flashed once again.

The man walked steadily towards her and, when he got close, pried open the arms that were wrapped across her chest. She surrendered to his every move. Her rain-sprinkled lips were pursed tight and showed no sign of initiating a sentence of any sort. But before long, on receiving tender contact from the corresponding part of the man, these pink pieces of flesh pulled apart. From there, organs of another kind tasted one another, sheltering beneath the roof of each other's mouth.

And then several other parts belonging to the two of them stroked one another, stuck, squeezed and squashed together, and scraped and scrubbed against each other until they were raw.

The rumbling and the roaring from above provided the soundtrack for the deed, appropriate for both offence and the defence.

The flickers in the sky manifested the rhythm of the mood.

From there, drip-drop, drip-drop, drip-drop, drip-drop, drip-drop, drip, drip, drip, drip… drip…

The last drop landed in a dark region, without witness.

The rain continued to fall from the sky, but the storm inside the couple's bodies had subsided.

The man stood up on his fatigued legs and left his companion's body lying still, steeped in a shallow pool of water that had collected on the concrete surface. A flash from the sky illuminated a certain body part of his, dangling beneath a tuft of thick, black hair. The rain trickled down over his body to the rounded head of the organ, then streamed onto the woman's left thigh like water from a tap. An instant later, he bent over to pull his underwear back up and cover the appropriate region.

Likewise, the woman took the opportunity to pull her shorts back on. She propped herself up on the flat surface, and the man held out his right hand for her to pull herself up.

The two stood side by side in the middle of the pouring rain, as though taunting the skies by their presence. They were face to face with the N and the O.

"There's something under the O," the woman remarked.

The man studied the black mass at the end of her line of vision.

"I think that something is a human body." Her voice quivered as she wrapped her arms around her torso once again.

"I agree with you. It appears to have arms and legs. It's probably a person, as you said. Why is there an inanimate body on my roof deck – and buried under not one but two giant red letters in such a cursed manner? The weight on the poor soul's body is not likely to be inconsiderable," the man reflected.

"What state is the person in? Approach and inspect."

The man broke the line of contact between the lovers, slowly moving his shivering body in the direction of the newly-discovered object. When the spark from above illuminated the nocturnal skies once again, he became certain that the object lying inert under the letter O was a male human being.

"The object lying inert under the letter O is certainly a male human being," he shouted, reiterating his thoughts to the woman.

The organ in her chest pounding, she followed her companion's footsteps.

"Is that unfortunate gentleman still breathing?" The woman's voice slipped through the curtain of rain.

"I'm unable to say as of yet. Patience, please."

The man tiptoed towards the outline of the body under the O. He squatted close to the ground and reached out to feel for an area on the stranger's body that might indicate some measure of life.

The sky's rod stabbed at the earth with a resounding boom.

The man under the O was lying facedown. His plaid shirt and jeans were soaked. His rubber flip flops had fallen off his feet, lying upside down not far from his body. The young man who did not wish to be named stuck the tips of his right middle and index fingers on the pulse point under the jaw bone of the prone body.

"No heartbeat is apparent. It's possible that this body is lifeless." He looked up at the woman, who had just joined his side.

"Who is he?"

The man used both hands to shift the head of the body, so as to be able to see the face more clearly.

The sky flickered three times in a row.

"He doesn't look familiar. His face doesn't register in my memory. It's the first time I've ever seen this gentleman." He contemplated for a moment. "What was he doing on this roof deck in the middle of a storm that's been blasting down like there's no tomorrow? Was he a criminal who suffered an unimaginable accident during the course of his professional duty – crushed to death out of nowhere by the letters from the advertisement sign?"

"It doesn't matter what he was. In a situation such as this, the first thing one should do is alert the police. Or else call an ambulance," the woman opined.

Her companion bobbed his head in agreement and got to his feet.

In the second floor bathroom, the man stood under the downpour from the shower head. The white tiles on the wet floor felt rough against the soles of his feet. The woman, now bone dry, lay under a soft powder-blue blanket. Her white T-shirt and dark blue shorts were slung on a plastic hanger, hooked onto the crank handle of a slatted window. The fan in the room spun a hundred and eighty degrees in each direction; one moment it blew on the surface of the wet fabric, another moment on the face of the woman on the bed. Her bare feet stuck out from under the blanket, creating an opening for the breeze to flow in and envelop her body. It was neither hot nor cold; the temperature in the room was more inviting than the weather on the roof deck.

The man switched off the squirting shower head, stepped out of the steaming enclosure and pulled a towel to his body. His rain-drenched clothes sat in the sink under the mirror.

Normally, at this juncture, people like to reminisce about the past, but the woman on the bed was pondering the future.

"When I'm exactly fifty-three years old, my son and daughter will both be grown up and have completed their education. My daughter's applying for a job at a big bank. My son's interning at a publishing house. He wants to be a writer, a poet actually, but his work's showing no sign of gaining recognition in literary circles. I stay home and do miscellaneous work because my husband's the general manager of a furniture export company. He earns a good income and can take care of the whole family. Nobody has to struggle. We have plenty of savings in the bank. There's nothing to stress about, so I only worry about the children's future."

As his hands twisted his wet clothes, squeezing the hidden water down the circular drain, the man called out from the bathroom:

"What's your husband's name? What does he look like?"

The woman smiled before answering. Even though the man could not see the expression on her face, he could surmise it from the tone of the voice that drifted into his ears.

"I greatly regret to say that it's not you. My husband's tall and dark. His face is roughly landscaped with hair. When I'm fifty-three, my husband will be fifty-seven. I met him while traveling overseas. I'd gone to visit a relative in London and stayed with her for some months, just enjoying the sights and sounds, enjoying being aimless. My husband was studying for a masters at a university forty minutes outside the city. He was a friend of a friend of a friend of the relative I was staying with. We met at a get-together for Thai people, got chatting, and hit it off. Not long after I returned to Thailand, he moved back here for work. He called me. We started going out.

One day, he asked me to marry him, and I said yes. He's a faithful husband who's devoted to our family – that's hard to find in this day and age. I'm happy I chose the right person. Our married life is serene. My mother passed away five years after I got married. She didn't get to spend a lot of time with her first grandchild. My husband asked my father to move into our spacious and comfortable home, and my father gladly accepted. Why live sad and alone when you can be close to your children and grandchildren? My father likes to garden. Soon after he moved in, my house became filled with brick-colored clay pots."

The man stared at his face in the mirror as he listened attentively to the woman contemplating her future. His fingers had become wrinkled like prunes. His body had come into contact with too much water for such a short space of time. The sound of the storm was ongoing; from inside it was faint, but one could infer that it was still fierce outside.

"You don't see me?"

The woman on the bed remained quiet through several flashes of lightning.

"Each to their own future. I don't see you around. We probably broke up a long time ago."

"When are you traveling to England?"

"Some years from now. About three years, I'd say. The day of the trip, I was really excited, having never traveled outside the country before."

"In three years. That means you'll have finished school."

"That's right, I've finished school. I couldn't find a job right away. I decided to visit my relative in London in order to scout things out, see if I could find a place to continue my studies. But the tuition there was unbearably expensive. My parents didn't have the means to send me."

"Please stop talking about the future. I don't want to hear about any future of yours that doesn't involve me. Let's just be happy in the present."

The man hung his wet clothes on the towel rack and walked into the bedroom. He was naked, save for the towel knotted at his waist. When he reached the side of the bed, he didn't look at the woman's face. He simply peeled the sheets up at one corner and lowered himself down.

"The police are taking their time getting over here. Twenty minutes have elapsed, and there's still no sign of them," the woman pondered.

"Rain. Traffic. Nothing unusual. They should arrive any minute now," the man said, slapping the pillow behind his head into place. He propped the back of his head up with his left arm, forming a barrier between the pillow and his hair. His right hand resting on his forehead, he glanced over at the television set on the wooden table three steps from the foot of the bed. The screen was silent.

"Shall we turn the television on and see what entertainment awaits us in the airwaves? There could be a drama series that promises to become addictive, or a game show that promotes the institution of celebrity, or an interview with a person of importance in society."

"Simply lying here is more peaceful. Don't forget the unbreathing body on the roof deck. There's a dead person in close proximity – how could have I have the heart to let myself be entertained by the media? I'm mourning that man's death," the woman remarked quietly.

The man tilted his face toward her.

"But who was this individual? He was no relative or friend of ours. For me to grieve and cry over his death would be poor acting. I cannot do it."

"I'm not grieving. But everyone who dies, no matter who they are, deserves equal sympathy. Apart from that, it's shameful that we were so oblivious. A dead person was lying steps away, and we still put on a salacious show out in the open without any consideration for earth or sky. Thinking about it gives me goose bumps. Disgusting." The woman contorted her face to display her sentiment.

"I'm starting to get goose bumps again. What would you say if I suggest that we…"

Before the man finished his sentence, the buzzer sounded through the whole house.

A few minutes later, the four-level townhouse contained several policemen and emergency workers.

"At approximately 21:00, while my female companion and I were amusing ourselves in our game of Twister in the bedroom on the second floor, we heard a loud bang from the roof deck. It was so loud and abrupt that it completely threw me off (almost literally, in fact). After hauling myself upstairs, I discovered that what sounded like the cracking of the sky came from the fall of two red English letters that were once part of an advertisement sign for a well-known brand of camera. Said sign used to be prominently placed on top of the neighbouring building. My companion and I were standing there looking at the massive letters piled on top of each other – and if you want a detailed statement, I can attest that one of letters was an N and the other was an O, and the N was lying on top of the O. We stood there in the middle of the rainstorm for a while, staring in bewilderment at the two letters, and then we noticed a foreign object lying motionless underneath the O. When we approached, it became evident to all four of our eyes that the object in question was the body of a man. I examined the pulse of the male victim and found no heartbeat, so I surmised that he had already departed this world. After my female companion and I paid an abbreviated version of our respects, I picked up the phone and requested you to come and investigate immediately. The unbreathing body of said man is still lying facedown in the same spot where the lady and I discovered him. So, without further ado, you should lead your team of men in khaki upstairs to execute your duty. If you'd like umbrellas to protect your crowns from the relentless downpour, I have some that you can borrow. Unfortunately, though, I only have two, so you'll have to share. Do accept my apologies for this. Please follow me to the stairs that will bring you and your crew to the roof deck, the scene of the incident."

"It's no problem about the umbrellas. We all have our own raincoats. But first, we need to ask you a few questions. It's protocol."

The young man led the team of gentlemen up the stairs.

"Are you the owner of the house?"

"No, my parents are the owners of the house, but they're on vacation. Right now they're probably sound asleep in a three-star hotel room somewhere in the south. I'm on housesitting duty. My female friend's staying here to help me watch the house, since housesitting alone is such an onerous task."

"Is it correct that you'd never seen the victim on the roof deck prior to this night?"

"I don't know him. I've never seen this man's face before in my life."

"In your opinion, what was the cause of death?"

"The cause of death is perfectly apparent. The unfortunate nameless man was crushed to death by the letters N and O. But how he came to find himself on this roof deck to be crushed by the giant letters, I haven't a clue. My own theory, which I told to my female friend, is that he might have been a criminal who suffered a tragic accident while carrying out a job. Whether that's correct, I do not know. I have to leave that part to you."

The investigating officer nodded in agreement.

The door at the top of the staircase slammed open onto the stage of the storm's light and sound show. All held up their hands to shield their faces from the splashing rain.

The lifeless body of the unknown man was still lying soaked underneath the O. The emergency servicemen approached. When they reached the body, two policemen and two medics together dislodged the giant letters and yanked the victim's body from under them.

"Seeing that my eyes have already grown accustomed to the image of this man's dead body, may I take leave to return indoors before I catch a cold? I hope you won't object."

To the beat of the thunder, the investigating officer nodded his consent.

In the second floor bathroom, the young man stood in front of the toilet. A stream of pale yellow liquid was passing from his own private faucet down through the U-bend.

"If that man wasn't a criminal, what other reason did he have for going up on the roof and making himself a sitting target?" Sitting on the edge of the bed, the woman yelled her question as she combed out her hair.

"I can't possibly be privy to everything that goes on on this earth. How am I supposed to answer your question?" Finishing his business, the man used the fingers of his right hand to shake the last drops off his personal tap before pulling his black underwear and shorts back up.

As he emerged from the bathroom, the sound of the official personnel's footsteps gradually pulled into focus.

Then a knock was heard on the bedroom door.

The man turned the doorknob and pulled it toward him. On the other side of the door, he encountered the sight of a stretcher being hauled out. The anonymous man's body was completely covered with a white cloth. The young man noticed a strange look on the faces of the officers walking past his door. Every one of them seemed to be turning to glance at him with disdain in their eyes.

The investigating officer stood dripping water on the other side of the rectangular door frame.

"I'm afraid the two of you need to follow me back to the station and fill out some paperwork, so we can officially open the case. It's standard procedure. It shouldn't take long."

The tone of the officer's voice was stern. The amiability displayed when they first met had vanished.

"Is something wrong? Why are you looking at me in that manner? I swear that my statement was truthful in every respect. My female friend and I really have never known or encountered the deceased. When we went up to the roof deck, we saw the victim lying lifeless under the giant letters, exactly as all of you saw with your own eyes."

"From our investigation, my colleagues and I believe your statement in every respect. Our theory indeed is that the hapless man lost his life from the forceful blow of those two enormous letters."

The officer paused to clear the phlegm in his throat. At the same time, the impetuous sky sent a threatening growl.

"But what my squad and I found utterly revolting was your shameless conduct. Even with a dead body lying there on full display, drowning in a puddle, you still felt the need to stage a love scene, in the face of a fellow human being's death. If the nation's young men and women are all as lacking in decency as you, our future will be be dark and dismal indeed. As a person of more advanced age, I'd like to express my sincere disappointment at the moral collapse of the younger generation."

The woman stopped combing her hair. Her cheeks turned bright red with embarrassment.

"But..." The young man's throat produced a strangled sound.

"Don't deny it. The smell given off by your flagrant behaviour still hangs in the air on the roof deck. It's so crude, even the purity of the rain finds it hard to wash away."

"But…" The young man was still trying to squeeze out a word.

"Let's drop it. Now please get dressed and follow me downstairs so we can wrap this up." The officer slammed the door in the man's face.

The young woman covered her face with her palms, obscuring the warm liquid that was starting to seep out behind them.

"How am I supposed to look those people in the eye? It's all your fault. I never want to see your face again."

Stunned, the young man remained standing motionless by the door. He knew in his heart that the sex act between him and his female friend happened before the discovery of the dead body under the O.

He was not guilty.

But how could he exculpate himself? The accuser was the flagrance in the air, that refused to respect the time and place.

THE DISAPPEARANCE OF
A SHE-VAMPIRE IN PATTAYA

Before she disappeared, she was spotted arm in arm
with a bald, burly Russian. At least that was the
rumour, picked up and passed on by the motor-
bike-taxi drivers who plied their trade at the entrance
to Pattaya Walking Street. But some of the local bar
girls recalled otherwise. *Russian my ass*, they said, *she
left with a boy, a skinny kid, eight years old, or maybe ten.*

The drivers were one hundred percent certain
that she was dead – murdered. They were willing to
bet that her body would have been hacked to pieces,
stuffed into a trash bag, weighted down, and then
tossed into the ocean not too far from the shore. The
bar girls, on the other hand, were convinced that
she and the boy had gone overseas. Maybe even to
Europe, to start a new life. *Good for her*, they said,
*human blood is all contaminated nowadays. There's no way
of telling what filth you might be drinking. If a vampire can
manage to quit the habit, she ought to get out of the game*

while she still can. Sure, people might say she's betraying her own kind, or even herself, but so what? Being a vampire in Pattaya isn't what it was. That's the long and short of it.

And the official line taken by the police? According to them, she'd never existed in the first place. And as someone who doesn't exist can't flee the country any more than they can get hacked to bits, there was nothing for them to investigate. *You'd have to be crazy to think we'd waste our time on a tall tale like that. If you're talking about the bar girls, the whores, the lady boys, the chicks with dicks, the go-go dancers, the drug dealers, OK, fair enough, them you'll find everywhere. As for the Russian mafia, let's both do ourselves a favour and leave that one well alone. But the vampires of Pattaya? That's nothing but a story people made up to keep their kids from straying too near the Walking Street.*

You're not going to buy that shit, are you? the elderly coconut vendor spat, his voice dripping scorn. *Of course she existed. She bought two of my coconuts. One for herself, one for her victim. She had a big heart, that vampire.*

No matter how widely opinions diverged as to the nature and cause of her disappearance, almost everyone maintained that she had been a creature of flesh and blood, and oh, what flesh and blood it had been! You'd have had to see her for yourself to un–derstand. Those dark eyes might stir up a shiver of fear but they also held you rapt, and not through any kind of sorcery, but because her beauty cast a spell of its own. When the wind caught her long black hair, it streamed out behind her like a piece of the night sky had come undone.

She wasn't a Pattaya native, and the local vampires considered her something of an upstart, a common bloodsucker encroaching on their territory. This was partly snobbery and partly envy; when it came to luring victims, she was far more successful than those who prided themselves on their authenticity, on employing only the classical techniques. Nevertheless, she won the respect and even the adoration of a small group of vampires from the younger generation. Already dazzled by her beauty, these impressionable youths were fully won over after she promised to always share her victims.

Her name was Rattika.

Though of course, this was all hearsay; anyone who claimed to have it 'straight from the vampires' mouth' was as full of shit as the police. Pattaya vampires didn't give interviews, and they weren't the types to get cornered for a chat. They were the ones who made advances, and those they did approach were unlikely to feel grateful for the attention.

If the drivers had it right, Rattika's murderer, the Russian, would have had to pretend to fall in love with her. He would have had to be a gang member, a contract killer. When the target was a Pattaya vampire, it wasn't just a matter of showing up for the deed. He would need the brains to devise an ingenious plan and the patience to then bide his time, waiting for just the right moment. He would have had to earn her trust. It wouldn't have been enough to convince her that he loved her – she had to fall in love with him.

Just as it was for humans, love was the Achilles heel of all Pattaya vampires. It had been a long time, perhaps hundreds of years, since Rattika had fallen prey to it. Her recent infatuation should have been seen as a a warning sign, a sign that she had walked right into a vampire trap. Poor Rattika, she shouldn't have let her guard down.

But if the bar girls were right, the story would have had an entirely different outcome, one in which Rattika and her son lived happily ever after, or at least were happy right now. If Ken really existed, as the bar girls were convinced, he would be a half-blood – half vampire, half human. Such things were considered scandalous in Thai circles, so the girls didn't dare raise their voices when they mentioned it. But they whispered, among themselves, and what they whispered was that Ken's father was a monk. That would explain Rattika's decision to disappear; she must have wanted to take Ken far away from the depredations of the vampire world, before he had a chance to be corrupted. He wasn't merely half human; he was half holy. Rattika would have wanted her son to grow up like a normal person, maybe even a good person. There was nothing good about the Pattaya vampire community. The bar girls claimed that Rattika and Ken had gone to live in a country where vampires were rare or even extinct. For some reason, they decided that Switzerland was the country that fit the bill.

Last week, a German tourist was out jet-skiing when he found a trash bag that had washed up on the shore. Inside were chunks of flesh. Autopsy results soon revealed that these were human remains, likely those of a child, who was probably male, and probably Asian. Other than that, the police had absolutely zero to go on in terms of identifying the corpse

The bar girls remarked that those chunks of flesh might well belong to Rattika's son, shaking their heads over the tragedy of it all, while the motorcycle drivers seemed disappointed that it wasn't the ravishing vampire herself. *But see? Someone got murdered exactly like we said.*

So where was Rattika now? There was no evidence that she'd been killed, and if the body in that trash bag was really Ken's, the notion that she'd gone to raise her son in a pristine, respectable country, unsullied by the taint of vampires, had to be abandoned.

The drivers tried to come up with an answer, but didn't have much luck. *Maybe she just took a vacation,* one of them sighed eventually. *If I see her, I'll let you know.*

SHALLOW/DEEP, THICK/THIN

There are no secrets in this world.

But once you leave this planet, secrets float in abundance, outnumbering scraps of meteorites many times over.

One fine day, a bit of secret the size of a thumb flew through the earth's atmosphere and landed in the heart of a forest reserve in this country's southern region.

A traveler stumbled upon that piece of secret from outer space, and his story spread by word of mouth to become front-page news all over the kingdom.

Reporters unanimously declared that a great discovery had occurred, but the traveler could not reveal what it was, because it was a secret.

People close to the lucky traveler bombarded him with questions about what the thing he saw was really like. The traveler would only shake his head.

No one saw that piece of secret again, but its fame continued to grow until it became a worldwide sensation.

Although the traveler announced to the public that he could not reveal the details of his discovery, the various media outlets would not relent. They persisted in pestering and pressing him for information, until he became an international celebrity, deprived of any privacy whatsoever.

He should never have gone and found that secret.

As the hounding escalated, the traveler reached the limit of his endurance. He decided to make an official television appearance for the whole world to question him.

Everybody waited eagerly for this live broadcast, which was to be a special program with no fixed duration. The producers, it was rumoured, would let the interview continue until the traveler caved and laid the secret bare to viewers. They would allow the broadcast to go on for days if need be. Advertising was not a concern because all kinds of brands threw their sponsorship behind the event – from the makers of sanitary pads to computer hardware, everyone wanted to get the secret out of the traveler.

When the crucial evening rolled around, everybody was sat in front of a television set, their eyes glued to the screen. Nobody did any work. Nobody so much as glanced at their homework. There were no sports. There was no gambling of any kind. There weren't even any robberies, murders or rapes. There was no war, international or civil. There was no stock trading. There were no religious ceremonies. There was no testing of weapons of mass destruction. There were no political sessions.

This live broadcast was many times more monumental than when the United States sent men to walk on the moon, because now a person walking right here on earth held an important key to the outer-space mystery that mankind had wanted to solve back then.

The studio was silent. Other than the producers and their team, no one was allowed in to watch the interview. They feared that if they opened it up to a live audience, things might get out of hand and have the place in an uproar. Every aspect of the event was carefully planned, even down to the pickup and drop-off of the new celebrity.

From the early hours of the morning in question, the traveler prepared himself physically and mentally. He got up several hours before the alarm clock crowed, notwithstanding that he had spent half the night lying awake with his arm on his forehead.

Before he could fall asleep, he'd had to concentrate on counting hundreds or maybe even thousands of sheep jumping over a fence; it had reached the point where the sheep themselves were on the verge of passing out from exhaustion.

The traveler had never suffered so much anxiety in his life. The more he thought about it, the more he resented that it had to be him. He was just a traveler in search of nature's beauty – he'd never asked to land in a mess like this. He could probably never return to the sort of life he'd used to live. Every time he set foot outside of his home, no matter where he went, there was always someone who recognised him. Everybody wanted him to spit out the secret from outer space. People made him all kinds of offers – money, gold, land, other valuable possessions. Some people even wanted to give him their sons or daughters. No one cared what kind of person he was, or what gender. No one ever bothered to ask his name, for that matter.

The traveler had plenty of stories from his life that he would readily share with the public, but nobody cared to hear any of them. The sole thing that everyone wanted to know was the one piece of information that he could not divulge.

Does no one want to know where my two feet have taken me? Does no one want to ask what I saw and what

I felt when I stood tall on top of a mountain high above the sea, or when I descended down into the miraculous darkness of the underwater world? And these eyes of mine? They've seen it all, from the wretched poverty of people who don't even have soil to eat, to the indescribable luxury enjoyed by billionaires, who have everything at their fingertips without having to getting out of bed. Does nobody care that I've seen several species of rare plants? That I've seen insects that've nearly vanished into extinction? That I've seen various freakish human rituals which, no matter how many times you witness them, are so bizarre you can barely trust your own eyes? I've encountered natural phenomena so beautiful it felt as though I was gazing upon heaven. I've also experienced those so violent and cruel it was like I was journeying through hell. A tsunami nearly engulfed me once. I've come this close to falling from a steep cliff, down into the abyss of death.

Just a thumb-size bit of secret — for me, it's nothing to get excited over.

What does it matter if you know the secret, when the whole point is that it doesn't want to be known?

Exploring nature's different. Nature always stands ready to welcome me. Whatever I want to know, I just have to walk over and ask, and I get an answer in no time, if not from a rock, then from a seed, if not from a blade of grass, then from the scent of mud.

I hold so much knowledge inside me, it's practically oozing out of my pores. Why does no one want to know what I know?

They only want to know about the secret. But what's so great about that?

The show's host was a familiar face on television. He was a middle-aged man, his head still densely covered with black hair that he wore parted on the left and held flat to the head with styling wax. That day, he was sporting a dark blue suit and a maroon tie. When the traveler stepped into the studio, the host made a beeline to greet him.

"A great pleasure. Don't be nervous. Relax. The program will start in just a moment."

He scrutinised the traveler from head to toe, and then one more time back up from toe to head: *Why did a guy like this have the good fortune to find the secret from outer space? He's dressed like a bum.*

The traveler was wearing a white T-shirt with the English words "Save the Whales" printed on the chest, above a pair of faded jeans. A pair of flip flops poked out beneath their ragged hems.

A smartly-attired blond foreigner walked over. The host smiled broadly as soon as he caught sight of the westerner.

"Let me introduce you. This farang is an American. He's going to sit with us and translate the interview into English for viewers around the world. He's very fluent in Thai." The host clapped the foreigner on the shoulder.

The American smiled and held his hand out to the traveler. "Hello. A great honour to meet you."

The traveler offered his hand in return, and the pair pumped each other's hands with sufficient vigour to demonstrate decorum.

"How about a bit of makeup? The whole world's going to be watching!" The host cupped his chin with his right hand, as if contemplating how to improve the appearance of his important guest.

"I don't think that's necessary," the traveler responded, his tone polite as always.

The host was still holding his chin.

"Yeah?" He sounded unconvinced. "Alright, alright, you can go on air just as you are, given that we don't have much time. It's almost ten thirty. Excuse me. I'm just going to use the men's room. Make yourself at home. If there's anything you want, just let the team know. I'll see you in a few minutes." Then he walked away.

The westerner waited until the host was out of earshot, then he turned back toward the man who guarded such an important secret. He whispered as though plotting some intrigue.

"I think I understand how you're feeling right now. Having the whole world's focus on you must make you uncomfortable. Come to think of it, it's not fair that you have to bear this massive burden alone. I feel for you. Still, I have to side with the others because I want to know the secret, too. So I want to make a plea to you: reveal the mystery. We don't want to waste people's time and make them stare at the TV screen any longer than they have to. Please. Think of the world."

"It's not easy to spit out a secret, but I'm going to try. My life is miserable these days. You have to understand that I never wanted something like this to happen to me. The sooner it's over, the better for me."

The foreigner nodded. "Please do try your best."

In the studio, a voice yelled out for all the participants to take their place.

It was more than ten minutes past ten thirty when the metaphorical curtains opened on the live broadcast that everyone had been waiting for. It began with the program's title and song then cut to a top-half shot of the host. The right-hand corner of the screen had a little rectangular area for the sign-language interpreter.

Tonight's duties in this regard had been assigned to a middle-aged lady in an emerald-green Thai silk suit.

The host put his palms together to wai the viewers through the camera. The woman in the small frame did the same.

"Good evening to our viewers at home. You already know why tonight's program is special." The host paused to flash a grin. The lady in the screen's corner was unsure what to do, so she attempted an equally suave, polished grin.

"He's sitting here with me now, viewers, the traveler who discovered the great secret in the heart of a well-known forest reserve here in our own country. For several weeks now, people have tried to contact him, this man, to inquire about his experience in the forest that day, but our traveler has refused to reveal the mystery, saying that a secret is a secret." Tickled by his own humour, the host interrupted himself briefly to laugh. The woman in the corner frame tried to find the correct sign language to convey that the host had succeeded in amusing himself.

"It's truly great news, viewers, that he changed his mind and agreed to be questioned in detail about that secret. I'd like to take this opportunity to thank our traveler for giving our program the honour of interviewing him tonight, on behalf of people around the world. Without further ado, let me introduce our famous traveler."

The camera zoomed out until all of the participants appeared in the frame. The traveler was sitting on a grey sofa, flanked by the show's host to his left and the blond westerner to his right. Each had a tiny microphone attached to the garment closest to his lips; the traveler's was clipped to the neck of his T-shirt.

"Hello." The host greeted the traveler with a wai.

The traveler waied back nervously.

"The foreigner who's with us tonight is an American who will simultaneously translate the interview into English for foreign viewers everywhere." Once he'd finished this introduction, the host stuck his right hand out to the westerner, missing the tip of the traveler's nose by just a hair.

"Hello. Good evening. Welcome." The host gave a burst of rapid-fire English while he shook the American's hand.

"Let's give him a moment to introduce himself to viewers abroad."

While the westerner was communicating with the rest of the world with words that sounded like *foot, fit, four, five,* the show's host smiled broadly into the camera. The traveler was sitting still but his eyes were darting back and forth. The lady in the screen's corner sat with her hands tucked away, staring blankly at the incomprehensible barrage of English.

As soon as the foreigner finished talking, the host hurried to keep things rolling.

"What a great thing that people around the world will be able to listen to tonight's historic interview all at the same time. OK, without any further ado, let's begin our conversation with our special guest." The sign-language lady resumed her duties in earnest.

"Mr. Traveler, we spoke a little bit backstage before we came on air. I understand that the main reason you've refused to reveal the secret you saw is its 'secretness.' In a moment, I'd like you to elaborate a little further on that point. But first, can you tell us briefly what the heck you were doing that led you to discover the secret from outer space?"

The westerner promptly translated the question. In the meantime, the traveler tried to search his brain's memory bank for this apparently extensive backstage discussion. When the foreigner finished talking, the traveler was still distracted and made no move to speak. Unable to bear any lulls in the conversation, the host quickly chimed in.

"According to the information I have, you were hiking in the forest that day, correct?"

The traveler nodded.

"And then you saw some kind of brilliant light radiating from a bamboo grove not far from the path you were following, so you decided to head towards it."

The traveler nodded again. He was more than a little surprised that the host knew the details of the story, as though he'd witnessed it with his own eyes. *How does this guy know about the bamboo grove? Did I tell somebody about it?*

"And then you saw it."

This time the traveler shook his head. "I didn't see it right away. The light was quite bright, which made it hard to see anything."

"It was *that* bright, viewers. What colour was the light, can you remember?"

"It…" The traveler paused to think for a moment. "It… It had no colour… It was white-ish and bright. That's it. It didn't have colour like electric light. It was more like an orb of light, like a small sun."

"And then you saw it."

The traveler nodded slowly. The westerner excitedly raced to translate.

Just as the traveler was about to open his mouth, the host cut in.

"It's truly riveting, this thing we've all been waiting to hear from Mr. Traveler's lips. The revelation is getting closer with each instant. But first, let's take a short break and meet the sponsors who made tonight's special program possible. We'll continue to solve the mystery after the break."

The team in the cutting room rolled the commercial footage, starting with an ad for engine oil, to be followed by a breath mints spot.

The host picked up a glass from the coffee table in front of the sofa and quenched his thirst with a swig of water. He gargled two or three times before swallowing all the water in his mouth down into his stomach. He turned to the traveler.

"Water?"

The traveler shook his head.

"Don't be nervous. You're doing great. The story about whatever light that was, was a surefire way to snag the viewers' interest. When we go back on air in a moment, you don't have to rush straight to the secret. Massage the viewers' curiosity first. Why don't you start with the general appearance of it, for example, the size, the color, the material, anything on our planet that it might resemble? And then act a bit scared, like you're worried that lightning might strike you down if you say something too directly, or something along those lines. The more you can stretch it out, the better. We have hundreds of commercials tonight. We have to manage the air time accordingly, so we can't let the program end too soon."

The traveler turned pale, like someone caught breaking the law red-handed. He turned to the westerner as if to seek his opinion, but the latter coldly shrugged his shoulders.

The producers signaled that they were about to go back on air. The host, the blond American and the sign-language woman each quickly straightened up and readied their camera faces.

"We're back. So we don't lose any time, let's continue our interview with Mr. Traveler." The camera zoomed out. The host leaned eagerly toward the traveler, who was now trembling in his seat.

"When we left off, there was a strange light coming from the bamboo grove, right? Once you got accustomed to the brightness, what did you see?"

His lips quivering, the traveler managed to say:

"I saw… something…"

"This something, how big was it? Was it large or small?"

"It was… small… about the size of a thumb." The traveler then held up his right thumb. The sign-language lady in the corner of the screen raised her own right thumb in response.

"Really! Viewers, the mystery that we've all been waiting to hear about is only the size of a thumb." The host bugged his eyes out for the camera before turning back to the traveler.

"And what else? This thing, was it a lump? A sheet? A ball? Or did it have some other unusual shape? Was it thick or thin? Long or short? On the surface, was it smooth, or was it ugly and eerie and rough?"

The traveler swallowed his saliva.

"It wasn't ugly... it wasn't eerie."

"It wasn't at all ugly or eerie?"

The traveler shook his head to confirm.

"In that case, was this mysterious object something beautiful?"

The traveler shook his head again.

"It wasn't beautiful either, viewers. It was neither ugly nor beautiful. This thing's getting more and more interesting. How fitting, given the fact that it's a secret from outer space." The host paused to adjust his suit jacket.

"Let me ask a stupid question," he said, flashing a quick smile into the camera.

"This secret, did it look mysterious? Did it have the appearance of something weird and mysterious?"

The traveler shook his head. His neck folded. He could only look at the flip flops on his feet.

Weird and mysterious? He could no longer remember.

After all, there are no secrets in this world.

The producers cut to the commercials.

THE SHARP SLEEPER

Morning. The sun was still low, flushing the earth's edges a juicy red. The sky, though not black, bore a smattering of gray cloud. Natee awoke, and as he was yanking his head up from his plush flame-orange pillow, he caught sight of a transparent button rolling off his stomach onto the wood floor by the foot of his bed, and slipping into a crevice between the slats.

He'd lost another button. This was the third one that week, from as many of his favourite night shirts. All three had fallen off at night, when Natee was sound asleep. In the matter of this button-shedding, at least three major possibilities existed.

One: Natee was, unbeknownst to himself, such a freakishly restless sleeper that he generated near-spark-inducing friction, causing the threads holding the buttons in place to fray unduly quickly. Two: one or more other hands were involved, and he was a victim of petty foul play. Three: the threads broke naturally, due to unavoidable wear and tear.

While all three theories were possible, Natee still lacked sufficient evidence to draw definitive conclusions regarding this puzzling case.

One — If Natee were that restless of a sleeper, why has no button-loss incident ever occurred before? He wasn't a kid anymore. It was almost ten years since he'd got his bachelor's degree. The cumulative hours he'd spent between going to bed and waking up, since his head was, as they say, the size of a fist (though his parents have never verified, and it cannot be proven, that his head was ever that size), were so many it was embarrassing to count. Even on nights when someone of the opposite sex had occupied the same bed (at the present time, several such persons have since managed to purchase beds of their own, while others have moved on to occupy the beds of people they're more compatible with), the friction generated never reached the point of slicing off a button. Natee had been involved in a bed-related accident only once, a long time ago. When he was not quite three years old, he fell off the bed. People often contended that he'd dreamed up this incident. ("Who the heck has such an amazing memory?" a university friend of his had exclaimed. "I can't even be sure I was alive when I was three. By the time I could remember anything, I was already in double figures, at least.

You hardly understand human language at three… or your parents, either. How do you know they're really your mum and dad? Do you really remember whose stomach you were kicking in? You couldn't even if you tried. It's pitch dark in there.") But Natee believed that it really had happened. It wasn't likely that it was a bad dream he was remembering. A child not even three years old wouldn't have much to dream about.

That morning Little Natee had suddenly felt a strange sensation by his lower belly. A millisecond later, he fell flat, facedown, from the bed onto the wooden floor. It made a loud thud. A moment later, he heard sluggish footsteps approaching.

"What happened here? How did you fall off?" a male voice asked in a flat, lifeless tone.

Little Natee was still lying facedown on the floor. Nobody cared to pick him up and put him back in bed.

"Very weird. The side of the crib is so high." This time it was a female voice, equally unexcited.

"Did he climb over it?"

"Is that possible? Look how small he is."

"He didn't even let out a cry."

"Do you think he injured his brain?"

"Don't know. I guess we'll know when he grows up."

"If he turns out stupid like you, then he must have done."

"Hey now, stupid isn't so bad. Nowadays, lots of stupid people make it to high places."

"Then why haven't you made it up there like the rest of them?"

"Because I'm not stupid, clearly. The fact that I haven't succeeded proves I'm smart."

The two quieted down for a moment. Little Natee started to feel like he was getting scrunched.

"Aren't you going to pick him up?" the male voice asked.

"You pick him up. I have a headache. I don't want to bend down."

A male sigh followed.

"My knees hurt."

"Just leave him like that for now. He's lying there so quietly, he seems to like it well enough."

Natee couldn't remember how long it was before he was picked up and put back in the crib. Sometimes he wasn't sure whether these events had really taken place, because once he was old enough to understand such things, he noticed that his parents didn't behave at all like the pair of voices that he remembered. They were normal parents, who worried about the well-being of their child no more and no less than other parents did. Nonetheless, Natee's memory only became more vivid over time, so it was hard for him to discount the truth of the story.

He asked his parents about it once, but both of them pretended not to hear him, which added to his conviction that his memory was perfectly accurate. In any case, that was Natee's only bed-related accident, and it had nothing to do with pajama-shirt buttons.

Two — If there really had been a second or third or fourth party involved, who had broken in to tear off his buttons as he slept, he'd be extremely surprised. The last human to have invaded his fifty-square-metre rented room and got within a hair's (or a thread's) breadth of him had voluntarily ceased such incursions several months ago. The spare key that Natee had made for said person had since been returned, neatly placed in a brown document envelope, together with a short note written on cutesy stationery, the kind with Japanese cartoon characters. The gist of the message was: too bad some couples haven't accumulated the same amount of good karma in their past lives, so they just aren't meant to be. One might interpret this as: some people were born to sleep on a bed that's too hard and too small to be shared for an extended period of time.

That night, after Natee finished reading that brief note, he immediately picked up the phone.

"That's it?"

"I only had the one key." The last human invader sounded a bit sleepy.

"I'm not talking about the key. I'm talking about us, our story. Isn't it a little too short?"

"Short stories are easier to read than long ones."

The woman was right. Natee has never finished reading a single novel. He put the phone down about as immediately as he'd picked it up. Immediateness is sometimes quantifiable, but hard to explain.

If it had been some other mysterious person or group that had intruded on his territory and snipped his buttons off, the culprit must have the ability to walk through doors, windows and cement walls, all without leaving a trace. If that was the case, Natee concluded, there was nothing he could do to rectify the situation. He'd simply have to submit to his fate, continuing to sacrifice himself as the victim of beings from the fourth dimension, because in a comparison of special powers (Natee can hold his breath under water for three minutes without coming up for air), he wouldn't make the cut. It didn't seem like a smart move to put his life on the line for a handful of buttons.

Three — Natee's three button-down pajama shirts, one pale blue, one banana yellow, and one communist red, weren't from the same era. The blue one was the oldest of the bunch. He got it as a New Year's present, which, if a detailed account were required, was two years, eight months and two days ago. The gift came from Aunt Urai, an actual blood relative of Natee's, whom the family had dubbed Aunt Millionaire owing to her being the richest of the lot. This wealth established her as an important person in the family, whom the relatives were keen to fawn over. Aunt Urai gave Natee clothing as a gift every year and for every occasion, except for Valentine's Day, for which she liked to give him something to slather over his gums instead: Italian chocolates that come in a bright red heart-shaped box. The blue pajamas from Aunt Millionaire were a brand named after a westerner who had stores bearing his name on various corners of the globe. In truth, not all of these stores were located on corners, and in fact, photographs from outer space have documented our planet earth as a round object akin to an orange, without any edges or corners whatsoever. Still, this westerner's name could indeed be said to be on every corner of the earth, because he had enough fame and fortune to change the shape of nature. It followed that whoever had the means to buy his merchandise as gifts for friends and family must have influence on a similar scale. Natee's Aunt Urai was one of those who were weighed on this same scale (which was sometimes heavy, sometimes light, depending on the other scales around, though those without the luxury of being judged on such a generously-weighted scale all felt that it was heavily rigged). Therefore, it can be conjectured that Natee's blue pajamas had been manufactured in accordance with the standard production procedure which is a fundamental factor shoring up the status of the prosperous foreigner. In accordance with the Western-language warranty, a button must not rupture under normal pressure. How could friction from everyday use cause it to fall off so easily, and after only a short period of wear?

The banana-yellow pajama top had a rather bizarre back story. It was a second-hand item that Natee had acquired inadvertently.

About a year ago, Natee's bosses assigned him to go and sort out an urgent issue in the provinces (the specific issue and province are superfluous to the matter at hand). When he arrived, he checked into the hotel that his company had reserved for him, which looked like your average three-star hotel (a somewhat undersized pool, bath towels that weren't as soft as they could have been). In room 3017, Natee opened the door of the white wardrobe to hang up his black suit jacket, only to find a yellow man's pajama shirt already hanging there. The previous guest had probably forgotten it.

Natee picked up the phone by the side of the bed and dialed zero.

"Yes." He flipped the key in his hand to check the room number, which he hadn't yet committed to memory. "I'm in room 3017. There's a shirt hanging in the closet. I think the previous guest must have left it behind." He looked out through the window. The afternoon sun clung soothingly to the run-down white building across the way, but Natee was no sun-worshipper, and the sight appeared somewhat intimidating to him.

The female operator on the line sounded as though she was chatting with one of her fellow operators. Natee could hear her snickering through the phone line.

(He he.) "What was that, sir?" (Ha ha.)

Natee repeated the sentences above.

"What kind of shirt is it?"

"I think it's a pajama shirt."

"One moment, sir."

One moment passed.

"Sir, the last guest in 3017 was from Taiwan. We probably don't have any way to contact him."

"Really? That's too bad then."

The operator started snickering again.

"Does it fit you?"

"Does what fit?"

"That pajama shirt." (He he he. Ha ha. He ha. Ha ha.)

"I don't know. I didn't try it on. Why?" The more he studied the sun outside, the hotter he began to feel.

"What colour is it?"

Natee glanced over at the wardrobe, its door still ajar.

"It's yellow."

"Is it a nice yellow?" (He ha. He ha.)

"It's a little pale, but quite bright."

"Is it yellow like a banana peel?"

(Ha ha. He. He he ha. Ha. Ha ha.)

"Something along those lines."

"If it fits you, you can just take it. We won't be able to send it back to the owner. Thank you. Is there something else I can do for you?"

Natee said no, thank you. He hung up, walked over to the wardrobe and stood meditating in front of it for a good while. He asked himself how much he liked the pajama shirt hanging in front of him.

Eventually, he started to find it endearing, like a starving puppy that had got separated from its owner and hadn't been fed for several meals. From that day on, Banana Peel had been a faithful pajama shirt to Natee. He imagined that it had completely forgotten its former master by now, so he couldn't believe that Banana Peel would allow one of its buttons to fall off just like that.

The communist-red pajama top, which, during certain periods of Thai history, would elicit a rather negative reaction from the majority if anyone had been sufficiently non-conformist to wear it, was the one that Natee was wearing on the morning in question. It was his newest pajama top, which he'd been inspired to seek out in the shops the previous month after a documentary about Mao Zedong had held him glued to the TV. Natee felt that if he had lived in mainland China when Mao was in charge, he would most likely have been one of the millions of Chinese people who put their faith in that broad-faced man's ideology. He even got misty-eyed while watching the documentary. Restless with enthusiasm, he was determined to leave the house right away and buy something bright red. The only communist-red thing that Natee had in his possession at that time was a plastic toothbrush, which was, in his opinion, a strictly personal item. It simply didn't demonstrate any sense of unity with society at large. No matter how sparklingly white and plaque-free his teeth were, the majority didn't share in the benefits. At least a comfortable pajama shirt helped people sleep soundly, and made, therefore, an important contribution to the prevention of societal unrest.

But finding a communist-red pajama shirt proved to be no mean feat. Natee spent several hours scouring various malls. Eventually he found one, at a big shopping complex in the city centre. (We won't specify the name of the mall here because Natee's not getting any kind of commission or compensation for promoting it. If the mall wants credit, please have a representative contact Natee privately.)

The red pajama shirt was sitting in a plastic box on a shelf, as though it had been waiting for him.

"Are you sure?" the sales clerk asked Natee as he keyed in the price on the cash register.

Natee looked up.

"Sure about what?"

"This shirt. Are you sure you want to buy it?"

"Why wouldn't I be?" Natee asked, annoyed.

"The colour's so flashy. It doesn't suit you. You seem reserved, polite and proper. If you wear this shirt, it might distort your personality."

"It's a night shirt. I'm going to wear it in bed."

"It can still have an effect. It might change your personality in your dreams."

Astonished and mildly irritated, Natee stared the shop assistant in the face. *Why is this idiot butting in on my life? It's my dream personality, not his,* he thought.

"Fine. It's your money. As long as you're sure, then it's none of my business. I apologise." (*Damned right it's none of your business,* Natee thought to himself.) The store clerk stuffed the shirt box into a shopping bag, took the money from Natee, and handed him the bag together with the change.

Natee has proudly worn the red pajama shirt several times since then, and his dream personality hasn't altered at all. On the contrary, the shirt has encouraged him to become a man of conviction in his waking life. As to what these convictions were supposed to be, Natee wasn't quite sure. But it was safe to say that a night shirt so principled wouldn't drop a button easily.

For these reasons, Natee was certain that his three favorite pajama shirts were absolutely not to blame for the button-loss phenomenon. Therefore, further investigation was surely needed to get to the bottom of the enigma.

Natee glanced at the alarm clock on the night-stand. The minute hand was between numbers three and four; the hour hand was pointing at number seven. He stayed sitting in bed, both hands resting over the third button hole from the top. The transparent button that had used to cling there would now be lying inert, wedged into the wooden floor.

On the wall to his left, the Chinese calendar – the kind where you rip off a page a day – showed number nineteen. The letters below the number read Saturday. He looked up from the red pajama shirt. For one long moment, he stared ahead like a person without a soul. When his spirit returned to his body, Natee lay back flat on the bed and let his head sink into the soft, plump pillow.

It was Saturday morning. Why get wound up over buttons?

SNOW FOR MOTHER

Beginning of November:

Nuan harboured a belief that she had never shared with anyone, not even with Aim, her regular hairdresser with whom she was so close they were practically family. But more than twenty years ago, her only son, Pon, had stormed into her mosquito net, his eight-year-old fists full of grass he had scraped up from the roadside. "Mommy, I brought you snow," he had announced to her in his little voice. From that day on, Nuan became convinced that if only her beloved son could come into contact with snow, real snow, he might be cured. She herself had seen them, those round white balls that resembled little taro dumplings, floating down from the atmosphere in colder climes, but only in pictures and on screen, never in person.

"It's such a strange disorder," Aim said, apropos of nothing, while washing her hands under the tap at the shampoo station. Nuan didn't pay much attention to her friend. It had been a topic of conversation between the two women for over a decade, and every time it came up, Aim felt the need to emphasise just how bizarre Pon's mental abnormality was, Pon who was now over thirty years old, but still brought his mother snow each and every day.

"Someone who's never seen snow, a kid who doesn't even know what snow is, how does he become fixated on it? It makes no sense." These are the same old comments with which Aim has tried to resolve the issue countless times before. "You said so yourself that you never put the image of snow into his head. You're not even familiar with snow yourself, are you?"

Aim didn't turn to look at Nuan as she posed the question. Her focus remained on the flow of water that was slipping through all ten of her fingers and washing the soapsuds down the drain. As for Nuan, she didn't let a word out of her mouth. She sat in front of the mirror, head tilted down to read the daily newspaper that she was holding open. Her fingertips were smeared with ink from the surface of the paper, so she grabbed a tissue from the flame-orange plastic box on the white counter below the mirror. She then rested the newspaper on her lap and tried to wipe the black marks off her tawny skin, until the thin white layers of the tissue had absorbed at least some of the ink. But the smudges remained visible; the ink had clung too closely to be wiped cleanly away.

"It's quiet today," Nuan said, before scrunching the tissue into a ball and tossing it into the waste basket. Aside from herself and Aim, no one else was in the salon.

"Yesterday was the same. It is middle of the week, you know," Aim shot back, as if she'd had the response prepared in her head. She turned off the tap and walked over to Nuan's seat with a wet washcloth in her hand.

"It's almost Pon's birthday again, isn't it? The twenty-fifth of this month, right?" Aim folded the washcloth in half before gently placing it on the base of Nuan's neck.

The warmth from the fabric quickly permeated Nuan's pores. She slowly nodded in lieu of words, then gradually allowed her eyelids to lower all the way down. The newspaper had been folded and placed in front of the mirror. Nuan tried to clear her mind in preparation for the massage her friend was about to pamper her with. Her shoulders happened to be tense.

"I have a good memory," Aim stated matter-of-factly as her clean fingers made contact with the reddish floral polyester that covered Nuan's skin.

The back of the salon chair reclined, and Nuan's body leaned obligingly back with it.

"Pon's birthday present this year is going to be the most special yet," Nuan suddenly confessed.

"I finally saved up enough money for plane tickets. For his birthday this year, his present will be his first trip abroad. I'm going to take him to Alasaka." Nuan kept her eyes closed all the while, carefully measuring every word that came out of her mouth, as though she were disclosing classified information to her friend.

Aim jumped with excitement. "Really, Nuan?" She momentarily forgot her duties, and her fingers pulled back from the customer's expectant shoulders. "Are you being serious?"

"Saving that amount was no walk in the park. At first I was worried that I'd be ancient by the time I had it down – even more ancient than I am now, that is – that I might not even live to see the day. Pon ought to count himself lucky to have such a dogged mother as me." Nuan opened her eyes and stared at the ceiling. The blades of the fan spun lazily, its rhythm perfectly in sync with the languid cadence of the music drifting in from outside.

"I like this song," Nuan remarked softly.

"Hang on a minute! You never mentioned a word about this to me. How much did you shell out?"

Despite her interrogation, Aim had an absent-minded expression on her face. Her attention was elsewhere, trying to visualise the scenery of the faraway land. Her hands began to maneuver back toward Nuan's collar bones. A-las-sa-ka. Alasaka. Alasaka. These four syllables meant nothing at all to her. She could repeat them without end, and she still wouldn't be able to imagine what the place looked like. Alasaka. A-las-sa-ka. At least the name sounded like it would be cold.

"Almost a hundred thousand for two, there and back. And then there's living costs for while we're there, and other expenses. That's why I said it was no walk in the park." Nuan gently closed her eyes again as Aim began to knead the pressure points on her shoulders.

"Wow," Aim exclaimed, though more out of politeness than amazement. Her mind was still occupied with the topography of the distant continent. "What the heck made you decide on this Alasaka place?"

"I've been planning this for a long time. I researched it myself and asked various people here and there. I was determined to take Pon to a place where there'd definitely be snow, and they say this Alasaka is seriously cold. It's so cold that there's always tons of snow, that's what everybody says. The books say it, too. I asked Ms. Jiu – you know Ms. Jiu the teacher, right? She confirmed that it was cold there, cold and very snowy. So I made up my mind that Alasaka was the place to take Pon. This way he'll see snow as soon as we get there, because it's all over the place, you know? You run into it just like that, so it'll be easy for him to get to see snow. But you have to fly more than a day to get there. And we have to stop somewhere else first, too. I'm a little concerned, it's true – I don't know if Pon will be able to sit still for so long, cooped up in that tiny plane all the way up in the sky. But I asked Dr. Sit, and he said it shouldn't be a problem."

"And how are you going to understand what anybody's tongue is saying? Or the other way around?" Aim couldn't think of a single instance during the course of their friendship when she'd heard Nuan whip up another country's – any other country's – language. She couldn't be 100% sure whether this was due to a lapse in her memory or because her friend had never done it in the first place, hence there was nothing for her to remember. But she suspected that the latter was more likely.

"I won't, probably, or at least not very much. I've been practicing, asking people to teach me, listening to TV programmes, sounding out the words on the page to myself. But I just ad-lib it, you know, just kind of take a stab at it. When it's for real, I probably won't have the nerve to open my mouth. Luckily, when Ms. Jiu saw that I was seriously planning to go, she went out of her way to find out if any of her students have family living in Alasaka. As it turned out, she eventually found one, a friend of an uncle of the sister-in-law of one of her former students. His name's Sompob. He works in a town called Fairbanks, so she suggested that I go there, as she'd already asked her student to send word to Sompob, and ask him to look after me and Pon. Ms. Jiu's network stretches so far! That's the benefit of having so many nice pupils. I really feel indebted to her." Nuan's jaw was aching from this lengthy elaboration. Her eyes felt irritated, so she went to rub them with her right hand. Aim quickly thrust out her own hand to intercept her friend.

"Pummel them like that and you're going to go blind before you get to see what it's like abroad. Huh!" Aim grabbed the warm washcloth from the base of Nuan's neck and used one corner of it to pat around her friend's itching eyes. "Ms. Jiu's fond of Pon. You shouldn't think of it as being indebted or anything like that. People who've known each other for decades, you do whatever you can to help, right?"

Below the nose on the face that was half covered with the white cloth, the lips were curling into a smile.

"It must be because of my good karma that I know quite a few nice people."

Aim pretended not to hear. She draped the towel back over the base of Nuan's neck and placed her palms once again on the muscles that were waiting to be kneaded.

"If your husband were still here, what would he say about his wife being so resourceful as to save a pile of cash, enough to take his son on an airplane to Alaska?" Aim snickered, her eyes watching for a reaction on her friend's upturned face.

If my husband were still here, I probably wouldn't get to go anywhere. And maybe Pon wouldn't get to go anywhere either. It's precisely because my husband isn't here that I pushed all the way to this point, Nuan thought to herself, without allowing any of these sentences to spill out onto her face.

When the faint strains of the song ended, Nuan glanced up at the ceiling fan again and began to move her lips.

"I'm excited. I don't know what's going to happen. I don't know what Pon's going to do when he gets to see, to touch, to scoop up real snow and hold it in his hands. But maybe some good will come of it. Maybe something will change."

"You think snow's going to help cure Pon." Putting her hands in the prayer position, Aim chopped lightly along her friend's shoulders.

The answer was yes. That was what Nuan was thinking and hoping would come of their travelling all the way to Alaska. She wanted to see Pon jump up and down on the snow and scream and shout with joy: "Mother! Mother, look! This is snow. This, this is what I've been trying to bring you ever since I was a child. This is what I've been searching for for more than twenty years. I've finally found it, Mother, I've found snow. Here it is. So much of it everywhere you look, you can sweep it up all you want and it'd never run out. I know everything I brought you in the past was all junk. I know it wasn't snow. Because today I can feel the coldness of real snow with my own hands. From here on, I won't have to keep on struggling to find it for you. This is enough. I can finally start living a normal life, like everyone else."

That scene would bring Nuan the greatest possible happiness, but she didn't dare set her hopes as high as her heart wanted her to, because she feared that if it didn't come true, the sadness would only multiply.

So Nuan told Aim: "I don't know. If that happens, it would be nice."

—

End of December:

"That cold?" Aim raised her voice to contend with the flow of water colliding with her friend's hair. The gooey honey-coloured shampoo in her hand was ready to be smeared and lathered on the scalp held over the ceramic bowl.

"I was numb all over, if you can believe it. I bundled myself up like sticky rice wrapped in banana leaves, but the cold still managed to seep in. Even gloves didn't do the trick. My fingers were so frozen I couldn't grip anything. My ears, my cheeks, my nose were all bright red as if they'd been roasted over a fire, but this was cold fire, and the only relief was to stand there with your teeth clenched," Nuan recounted happily. She kept her eyes shut tight to prevent water from splashing into them.

Her body was stretched out straight on the plastic-upholstered bed, every muscle relaxed.

"People there are nice. They're friendly. A lot of families fish for a living. They go out fishing even though it's so cold. Hard to believe they can bear it. I met a nice American girl, probably not even twenty years old. Her name's Abby. Sompob introduced us. He told me she was raised in an orphanage as a baby. When she was a bit bigger, a couple from some desert state asked to adopt her. The weather was the polar opposite to Alasaka. The desert's hot, you know? She lived there for a while, and then it turned out the husband was a psycho. He liked to beat women or something like that. Abby put up with it until she was grown up, but eventually she couldn't take it any longer. She probably got mistreated too often, so she packed her bags and took off. She just upped and walked out of the house one day. And then she hitchhiked her way around the country until she decided to settle down and find a proper job there in Fairbanks. And do you know what she does? Her job is to move fish in and out of freezers. Imagine it – a young girl, not very big, carrying blocks of ice up by the North Pole. The whole city's like a freezer already, you know? And on top of that she works with cold, clunky stuff. She's really tough. And she's sweet. She'd chat with me about this and that. I just nodded along." Nuan's giggles interrupted her speech. "I had to wait for Sompob to relay the trans-lation. It was a lot of back and forth before we could understand each other. But it was fun. I really like that kid. Don't know what she was thinking running away to a freezing place to do freezing work. But I'll tell you something, she seemed happy."

Aim didn't pay much attention to the story about the amazing American girl named Abby. Her frustration was too great. How much longer was Nuan going to go on and on about this nonsense? Although she was delighted to have her friend back in this hemisphere, what about the crucial purpose of her intercontinental travel? Its outcome was the subject Aim was eagerly awaiting, the subject Nuan showed no sign of approaching.

Nuan's hair had become much coarser, probably due to the dryness of the air in A-las-sa-ka. "What about the food? How was it? Could Pon eat anything?" Aim tried to steer the conversation toward her own target.

"How should I put it?" Nuan took a moment to reflect on her own question. "Their food's just not really to our taste. It's so rich, so bland, and not very appetizing. Granted, it does help make the cold easier to tolerate. Once you think of it that way, you can eat anything. Some days it was even quite tasty. Especially hot tea – that became my favourite thing. You know yourself, when have I ever liked tea? But the weather was so brutal that to get a break from the cold and sit in a little café sipping a cup or two of hot tea just cheers you right up. And now I've brought my tea addiction back with me." Nuan let out a laugh that interfered with Aim's conditioner application. "But tea's not exactly food, is it?"

Why isn't she talking about the snow?

Nuan herself was fully aware of what her friend was waiting for.

On the inner surface of her eyelids, the images from her freshly minted memory were projected.

Pon was stamping over the dazzling white ground. His eyes glittered and gleamed as though beholding some great wonder. After he snapped out of the reverie, he bent down to gather up snow until each palm cradled a handful. Then he approached his mother, who was keeping a close eye on her dear son's every move.

"Mother, I brought you snow." The thirty-one-year-old man's boast was delivered in a voice oh-so-familiar to his mother's ears.

"Thank you, sweetheart," Nuan said as she reached out to accept the mounds of icy crystals. A cloud sprang from her mouth after each word.

It was the same phrase with which she had thanked her son every day since that first time over twenty years ago, the same phrase she would likely have to go on repeating tomorrow and the next day and the next.

How many mothers out there...

...get to say thank you to their child as often as I do?

MARUT BY THE SEA

Before it's too late, may I tell you, dear readers, that my name is not Marut? And I'm not sitting by the sea at all. If you want me to confess, I must admit that I don't know my own name or what kind of landscape surrounds me. I might be standing in front of a train station. I might be walking through an untamed jungle. I might be sleeping in a spaceship that's traveling to a faraway galaxy. The possibilities in that regard are limitless. I'm sorry – I might not even be a person. You might be reading the confession of a bogie. Who knows?

There's this guy. He likes to think that he knows it all. He bosses people around, dreaming up their destinies as though he were God. To make matters worse, deep down in his unconscious he secretly believes that he's so smart, that he's a top-notch philosopher in a class of his own, that he's attained all the Noble Truths of Buddhism, that his enlightened mind perceives all nature's intricate cycles, that he gives life and breath to cows and buffaloes that he moulds out of clay, that he can shape stories out of nothingness. Well, watch out. He's a major con artist. Don't waste your precious time with his nonsense. Granted, he might say or do things to amaze you. He might write words that tug on your heart strings. You might find his unusual perspective charming. He might lead you to believe that he has something important to say. But believe me, every single thing that you think you learn from him in fact comes from you yourself. As the Thai expression says, grandma's treats bought with grandma's money. That's all it is. People like him are the most dangerous of all. He dangles your own humanity in front of you for you to buy. The more you fall for it, the more influence he has over your brain cells. Eventually, one day, without your knowing it, every sentence that passes through your head will have him as its puppet master, operating behind the scenes.

You have to count yourself very lucky that you're reading my exposé. Let me tell you something – but don't pity me once you've heard it – because it's bound to happen sooner or later.

I won't be able to continue with this exposé for long. Any moment now, I'm going to vanish into thin air. And we shall never meet again. Therefore, you ought to make the most of your time with me. It's all to your own benefit.

Prabda Yoon, whose name appears below the pathetic and untrustworthy title at the start of my exposé, that's him, that's the guy I'm talking about. He's the one who upped and decided that my name was Marut. He's the one who wants to order me to sit by the sea. He probably thinks the title is so snappy. "Marut by the Sea." Stop, please, before I fall backward laughing. Did you know that when the incomparable Mr. Prabda dreamed up this title in the brain that, in his head, is truly massive, he still had no idea what the story was going to be about? Now that you know, what do you think? Your opinion can't be too far off mine. That's right: this guy's a scammer!

OK, just for fun, as an experiment, let's help this Yoon brainstorm. Suppose my name is Marut and, for whatever reason, I have to sit by the sea. What should my emotions be while I sit and stare at its waters? Maybe I feel lonely. That's the easiest feeling, either lonely or sad. People go and gaze out at the ocean in order to let go of unhappiness, don't they? It's such a huge amount of water. And salty to boot. It correlates with the amount of sorrow that's flooding the watcher, eroding their heart with a saltiness that's hard to cure. How's that for a story? It's bound to excite a reaction in one or two impressionable people. Moved, these people fall prey to Yoon as they read, and become his emotional slaves. It's that easy.

Or, if we want to give Yoon a little more credit, maybe he's not the type to dream up something so simple. Suppose the story is more complex, full of artistic and linguistic refinement (yeah, right). Suppose we don't know who Marut is. He's not even the protagonist of the story. Let's say the real main character is a child (to give the impression that Prabda is fond of children). Let's say it's a boy named Asshole. (Oh, he likes these unusual names, all right – anything to get your attention). Befitting his name, the kid is a surly rascal. He doesn't listen to his parents. If his mother so much as touches him, he kicks her. If his father dares to pet him, he gets a slap for his pains. Little Asshole wins the award for the nation's most ungrateful child. Then, one day, his parents couldn't put up with it anymore. They decide to stuff their evil child in a sack, throw him in the boot of the car and find some quiet stretch of sea to send him floating far away, out of range of their eyes and ears. When they reach the seaside and complete their intended business, they get back into the car and prepare to drive home. Suddenly, a man walks by their car. It's none other than Marut. He strolls along until he decides to plonk himself down on a spot of sand. He looks straight out at the horizon. To have Marut sit by the sea, that's all we need.

Believe me, Prabda's stories don't get any better than this. I myself could write ten or twenty a day. But I might kill myself first – it's too easy. The examples I brought up are his specialty. In other words, the type of bizarre story which he makes end so cryptically, as though the harder it is to understand, the better. If you try asking Sir Yoon what the meaning of each of his stories is, believe me, he'd chuckle deviously, *heh heh*, before answering, "Why don't you try asking the stories themselves?" Or else, "The meaning? What do you think the meaning of your life is? The meaning of my story is the same." Or, "If I knew, why on earth would I write?" Or, "Not knowing is the purest knowledge." Listening to that makes me want to strangle him until his eyes pop out of their sockets. People of that sort deserve to die, nothing more.

Do you know the kind of problems they have, those people who are writers or call themselves writers? Oh, they have a lot of problems. They're the type who've had trouble integrating into society ever since they were children. They think everything is terrible. Ugh! They'll pass comment on all sorts of things – from the cleanliness of tap water to religious wars between extremist factions. They act as though they know it all because they're terrified that people will think they're dumb. They can't stand to be labeled as stupid. Why? Because they hate stupid people to the core. They complain day and night that world civilisation is deteriorating. But who do you think is making it deteriorate? People like Prabda are at the heart of it. Not only do they fail to make themselves useful, they create nothing but negative sentiment, a deadweight that is piling up thicker and thicker over time and burdening society. One day, it'll cause us all to sink into the ocean.

Prabda, he acts as if he's easygoing. He wears T-shirts and simple trousers, strolls through the streets trying to look as down to earth as possible. People like him sometimes sport the traditional garments of some local tribe or another, as though they're advocating some kind of phony cultural preservation. But if you dig deeper, you'll find most of them have nothing whatsoever to do with the culture in question. It's largely trend-following; the only culture on show is that of the tribe of corny artists. Its chief perpetrators are those who like to prop up bars from evening through to morning, preaching at the younger generation. These people should have all their teeth yanked from their gums, then the pulled teeth should all be placed in a glass case and exhibited as a cautionary tale, so the public will realise the true cause of civilisation's decline.

You might have a book (or several) that you cherish, that will always have a special place in your heart. It might be a book that made you cry your eyes out. It might be a book that made you laugh. Or it might be a book that gave you hope, that inspired you to continue living your life. Readers, believe me: take that book out of its special place in your heart and burn it. Don't let a few hundred sheets of paper, a few cartridges of ink, a few hundred thousand letters (or even a few million) put boundaries on your life. You should comprehend by now, given my elaboration thus far, that whoever wrote that book dearest to you is no finer a human being than anybody else. He has no clue what he's done. Do you know how I got the opportunity to pop up and communicate with you today? It's simple. Prabda hasn't come up with a plausible reason for why Marut is sitting by the sea.

You might be thinking that I'm part of his genius. Don't. You might be admiring him, thinking that he has creativity to spare. That he uses deep, strange ideas to write stories that are complex and layered. Honestly, I'm not a character he created. He never intended for me to be fooling around on this page.

And as soon as he sees what's happening below his fancy title, I'll disappear from this world of letters. No way will he let me continue to roam free.

Don't think I'm scared. I actually want him to deal with me as soon as possible, so I can finally escape from this worthless situation. I can't stand playing a part like this in the imagination that fools the world. The quicker he gets rid of me, the better. Hey! Come on, buddy! Yoon! This way! I'm here, jerk! Can't you hear me, you dummy?

I guess he's still sitting with his brain empty somewhere. So pathetic, don't you think? He thinks he wants to be a writer, to move ideas from the world of imagination through writing. He can barely move faeces through his rectum, never mind imagination.

While we still have some time, why don't we help Prabda think about how he can improve his life? Is it possible for him to keep doing what he does, but with a purer heart? What can he do to stop deceiving people?

First, I think he absolutely must admit to himself and society that he's stupid. Yes, his IQ is no higher than a duck's (which is a reasonable IQ since ducks, as far as birds go, have pretty decent ideas), and he has no right to inflict the few thoughts that he does have on hapless bystanders. No, I don't want him to sit at home doing nothing. He should spend the majority of his time sweeping public roads, watering plants under elevated highways, or wiping windows around the city until they're sparkling clean, before he applies himself to the task of moving whatever it is through whatever channel.

How do I know Prabda is stupid? Of course I know. I've known him since his brain was just developing. Did you know that Prabda likes to tell anyone who'll listen what a passionate devotee of literature he is? But does anyone know how many books he's actually finished reading? Oh, the number isn't that high in the double digits. The ones he really remembers are even fewer. He might talk the talk, like he knows a whole slew of important works. In all seriousness, if you made him take an exam to test his knowledge of the world's influential literature, he might be able to answer two or three questions tops. The rest would be pure waffle, just as he's waffled his way through life since he was a kid. He might be able to namecheck plenty of authors – especially those whose books are known to be 'difficult'. Why? Because he knows that the more challenging the book, the fewer the people who've made it through it. It's a crafty strategy to cover up his ignorance. This is a sad fact that he has to face and accept before he can hunker down and create more work.

You might be thinking to yourself, why do I hold such a grudge against this young man? Oh, I'm no more interested in him than I am in dust particles in the air. But whenever I get the chance to come out and expose what I genuinely know, I have to use the time as wisely as possible. No matter what, Prabda has more influence than I do – he's out there; I'm in here. At the end of the day, I can't compete with him. When I see the opportunity to exert some influence, I have to make the most of it. Don't hold it against me. You might even come to want to thank me at some point. I might be opening your eyes, be it a lot or a little.

I don't even want to think about how Prabda's future will turn out if he keeps behaving the way he's acting now. Oh readers, let's help him out a bit. Don't let him wallow in his false beliefs. Let me tell you, he thinks he's free, at least in terms of thought. That's what he said. I'll tell you for your own good: (you all should heed this, too, because there are many among you who think as Prabda does) freedom, whether physical or mental, doesn't exist. Physically, everyone is a slave to the air, the sun, water and food. Mentally, the majority at least are slaves to language, culture, tradition, *etc.* People's servitude is so *et cetera*. So don't make me laugh by saying that you're a free thinker. Do you want me to prove it to you?

The appendix.

You see only *that*, and yet your mind can't help but follow along. Everyone knows the word "appendix." You think whenever someone utters the word "appendix," you know for sure what the person is talking about. But how many times in your life have you seen an appendix? Some people may never have seen one at all. Nevertheless, you're convinced that you know what an appendix is. That's enslavement to language. It creates an image in your head, even though you've never had any first-hand experience of what's behind the word. Don't let me bring up the head or the heart. Otherwise it might get too deep, and we'd venture too far into Prabda's favourite territory.

I know that I'm wasting my energy, that the outside world to which you all belong will ultimately continue its course as before. What can I, myself, do to fix it? Prabda will continue to be besotted with his own imagination. But I'm praying that at least he doesn't become any more successful than he already is. Please, may more and more people discover his true colours, and turn away from every single one of his letters. Then who knows, he might finally go and do something that's actually useful. I still maintain that he could do worse than sweeping the streets, for a start.

There. I feel Prabda's imagination creeping near. My surroundings are starting to grow colourful, to acquire shape and form. I'm starting to see the outlines of myself. OK, come here, stupid! You can fool other people, but you can't fool me. Here! Do what you want with me. Give me my face, layer on my personality as you will. Construct whatever storyline for me you please. I'm always ready. At least I got to use the time up until now to humiliate you. That's some satisfaction. Oh, it's here. A square frame. A white box. Don't tell me – it's a room! Oh! If only I'd bought a lottery ticket, I would've won the jackpot. It really is a room. What kind of room is this? Purple curtains, how passé. There, a window's popped up. A table, a chair, a bed, pillows, bed sheets, a blanket, a lamp, a door, a phone, a mirror, a TV. Hey, you! Why such an old model? A wardrobe, a refrigerator. Oh, there's even a picture on the wall. How much are you going to promote the arts? Don't tell me this is a hotel room. There, there's a white towel draped over the back of the chair, too. Ooh! There's even a balcony. Not too shabby. Aaah, my body is starting to acquire flesh and blood, dear readers. In a second, my face will appear. In a second we'll know…

My name is Marut. What I see through the window in front of me is a boundless ocean.

The indigo water stares, unblinking, at my face.

THE CRYING PARTIES

The same room was no longer the same. The carpet had stayed the nasty shade we'd nicknamed "upchuck green," and traces of our memories remained on its surface in the form of faint blotches, resembling a perfect mélange between abstract art and a pile of vomit – strictly speaking, we ought to call it "realism," as what looked like puke stains really were.

In those days, when we used to organise a crying party every week, the four of us would frequently throw up on that carpet. Our stomachs couldn't handle June's brutal cocktail recipes. She claimed to have enrolled in a "Creative Cocktails" course at one time. We didn't really buy that. In our opinion, her 'inventive' recipes were bound to kill somebody someday.

"Stop exaggerating," June would object. "I create art, not poison." June was quite proud of her artistic spirit.

It was a rented studio apartment in a tall building that poked stiffly up, like a concrete phallus, on a boisterous corner of Bangkok. June had moved in when she was a third-year in university, the reason being its proximity to the campus. After she graduated, she stayed loyal to it, though she could have easily shifted to a fancier place with her five-figure salary.

She worked as a copywriter at a well-known advertising agency. "The work of a copywriter like me is copying the work of real writers," she liked to quip, then cap the statement with a roaring laugh. We couldn't help but join her in a chorus of laughter to amplify the sound of her happiness.

June's favourite form of humour was self-mockery, for which we provided plenty of ammunition. Whenever she was down, no matter for what reason, instead of consoling her, we'd usually ambush her with even harsher stuff, then end with: "Goodbye, June, we know you're going to go home and kill yourself. See you in hell." June would smack us hard on the back and grin.

But the last time we said to her, "Goodbye, June, we know you're going to go home and kill yourself. See you in hell," June went home – to this room – and really did kill herself.

I couldn't eat anything for several days after I heard the news. I was constantly nauseous. We all turned into zombies for weeks. Who could believe what had happened? I hoped not to find June in hell when we landed there; I hoped she'd been permitted to go to a better place.

A new tenant had moved into the apartment. He was an IT guy straight out of the nerd copybook. His name was Lert, and he probably wasn't more than two or three years older than us.

Lert knew before he moved in that a woman had committed suicide in the apartment, but the rent, which the landlord was forced to reduce by almost half, encouraged him to ignore the spooky atmosphere. He wasn't particularly concerned anyway. Lert talked a big game, saying so what if this room was haunted by the ghost of a young woman? Young female ghosts held no fear for him. He told me on the phone that he had a secret charm especially for shooing away ghosts, but he wouldn't say what it was; when we eventually set eyes on him, we guessed that it was simply his face.

Oh, Tae, Num and I had made plans to party this evening when we bumped into one another at a friend's wedding a few weeks ago. We all worked full time now, so we didn't hang out that often. But whenever we did see each other, what leapt into everyone's mind at the same moment was June and the crying parties.

—

We all missed June dearly, but we didn't miss each other that much. Our history was, we kind of hated each other's guts. We'd started to hang out together for one reason only: we were each infatuated with the same girl.

The four of us began as enemies. June wasn't pleased when she realised that she was the cause of our feud.

"You four should call a truce," she suggested. She then convened a meeting so a ceasefire could be declared. It was a miraculous and commendable act – we were a group of pathetic males just itching to fly at each other's throats, yet one woman managed to turn foes into friends. I had no clue how it happened, but June handled it effortlessly. All she said was, "Let there be peace," and there was peace.

The sad part was, June wasn't in love with any of our crew, which was probably why she felt at ease hanging out and partying with us.

It took me a fairly long time to come to terms with that fact. We all needed quite some period of adjustment before we were able to have fun, messing around with one another at the crying parties.

—

"What? A crying party?" Lert had been baffled at first, when I spoke to him on the phone earlier in the week. I'd contacted the building to ask who'd moved into June's apartment. The employee who answered the phone put me through to Lert, I introduced myself and told him about June.

"Oh, the woman who killed herself in this apartment?" Lert's voice was so flat it was as if he was talking about somebody crossing the street when the cars had stopped at the red light – oh yeah, her, the person crossing the street.

Yes, that was June. I continued by telling him that three friends and I had a favour to ask. We wanted to use his place to throw one final crying party. We were prepared to let him do background checks and look at our national IDs, or to provide any supporting evidence that would make him trust in our good intentions. We were happy to let him stay behind and act as our chaperone, or even join in with the party, if that was what he wanted. It was all fine by us.

"You all met up here every Sunday to get drunk and eat raw bird's eye chilies until tears came out of your eyes? And you competed to see who could cry the longest and the most? That sounds ridiculous... and kind of awful," Lert opined after I'd finished explaining the gist of the crying parties to him.

He seemed to have a good grasp of it.

—

It's probably no great revelation to say that June was the one who instigated the crying parties. As I understood it, she founded them on a day when she was dealing with some form of heartache. But June didn't breathe a word of this to us – she even acted particularly cheery when she opened the door to welcome us to the first gathering. As time passed, we gradually uncovered for ourselves that the crying parties weren't organised merely for our entertainment; rather, June used them as a way to detach crying from sadness.

She wanted to train herself to cry for amusement.

The four of us began to fathom June's behaviour not long after the crying parties began, but we didn't care. Getting to have these special moments with her every week meant far more to us than whatever private motive she might be harbouring.

Before we knocked on June's door, the four of us would go pick up the provisions together. The selection of the chilies was no less crucial a step than chomping them down. Only rarely can anyone have picked out chilies as meticulously and painstakingly as we did. The vendors would regard us with question marks in their eyes.

"I'm not sure..." Lert said into the receiver. "Why should I let four male strangers use my place as a venue for chili worship?"

I proposed that we pay him, as if we were renting his room for a few hours.

He accepted, under the condition that he would stay in to monitor our conduct.

Hence we were here, now, Sunday evening, around half past seven.

Lert had inherited some of June's furniture, that her family had abandoned there. Along with the hideous green rug, her grey sofa and coffee table were just as we remembered them. I didn't know if the landlord had notified Lert of the history of the stuff in the room. Did he know that June's heart had stopped beating on that sofa?

Num was the first to lower himself down onto it. He stared blankly at us, and then Tae walked over to sit next to him. The sofa wasn't large enough to accommodate four people comfortably, so Oh and I sat down on the carpet. I placed a yellow plastic bag stuffed with red and green chilies on the table in front of us that had Lert's computer magazines strewn all over it. As soon as Oh set the bag of beers down, Tae reached in for a can.

We each felt parched.

Lert had his eye on us as though he were expecting something shady. He stood stiff as a statue in front of the TV in the corner of the room. "You guys are going to sit and drink beer and eat chilies until you cry, and then you're going to leave – right?" Lert asked, stepping a little closer to us.

We nodded in unison. I pointed at the chili bag and asked, "You want some?"

"No, thanks."

"We won't stick around long," Tae told him, taking a sip of his beer. "We'll probably wrap things up by nine."

"I hope so," Lert said. He looked concerned, and also like he didn't know what to do with himself. It was as though the room belonged to us again – no, not to us, to June.

"I don't know how I agreed to let you all come here," Lert said. "I think this whole operation's too wacky by far."

The four of us looked at each other. Num reached inside the bag of chilies, extracted a bright red specimen and bit half of it straight off.

The crying party was thereby officially in session.

"You should join in," I encouraged Lert. I was trying to find a way to help him relax, both mentally and physically. "The release of tears without sorrow or pain is a really interesting sensation."

"Interesting? I think you're all demented." Lert refused to loosen up.

"I've changed my mind. It's making me uneasy, having a bunch of strangers sitting around in my room. I have to ask you all to leave right now." I heard the quiver in his voice. It seemed he'd had to summon a good deal of courage before he could open his mouth to kick us out – in his eyes, chili eaters must have been mighty intimidating.

"We can't leave yet," Tae said sluggishly, complete-ly unperturbed. "The party's just started. Don't worry, we're good guys. We're harmless. We just want to finish our party, and then we'll go. In the meantime, feel free to do your own thing."

"But this is my apartment! I have the right to kick you out. Please pack up and leave, or else I'm going to have to call security," Lert raised his voice more. His face slowly turned red. I sensed that he genuinely wanted to call security.

We looked at one another again. Oh and Num's cheeks were already drenched with tears. Apparently they'd gobbled the chilies down in a hurry. Meanwhile, Tae's tears were welling up, and I myself was starting to feel the power of the spiciness build up inside my nose – I'd eaten only a single chili, but, as I had the weakest tongue in the group, I was sure to start crying soon.

—

"I said get out of here! Didn't you hear me?" Lert was really becoming a nuisance. We consulted with each other in silence. Four pairs of soggy eyes posed the question: *How are we going to shut this idiot up?*

When he saw that no one was heeding his order, Lert walked straight over to the white phone hanging on the wall next to the kitchen area. "I'm calling security up here right now," he threatened.

"Hey now… cool off a little, won't you? You can see that we're not doing anything bad. We're just sitting here eating chilies, for fun," Num said. The voice that came out of him sounded distinctly like a snivel.

"Go eat them somewhere else," Lert argued.

"But this is the only place where our crying parties can happen," Num explained. His words were becoming increasingly difficult to decipher. "And we paid you the rent as agreed."

"I don't want your money anymore. I just want you all to leave my apartment, right now!" Lert picked up the receiver.

—

I was crying.

I sipped my beer and looked around the room through the veil of tears. Then I tilted my head down and stared at the stains of memories on the surface of the rug. My tongue felt swollen and numb. The others were probably experiencing similar symptoms. Each of us scanned the room, in search of June's eyes.

"Security's on the way up," Lert said, with the bold voice of a winner.

We went on sitting there in silence, continuing to eat the chilies.

The four of us weren't exactly dear friends. We were starting to realise only now that we hadn't actually wanted to come here – but we would stay and cry until we were dragged out of the room.

We were waiting.

Waiting in the same room that was no longer the same.

We tried searching for June in our good-time tears.

But we didn't find her.

We only found that our tears weren't tears of amusement.

FOUND

"He's disappeared," Duan hollered, her voice nearly swallowed up by the sound of the waves.

"But he promised," I yelled back, feeling irritated. Duan nodded in agreement. Then she stamped her way further along the beach, still hoping to find the middle-aged fisherman.

Dusk was approaching. Everyone on the beach was awaiting the special night. Tomorrow, the people of the world would wake to greet the final year of the twentieth century. Even though it was none of Buddhists' business, our nation got caught up in the excitement along with everybody else. Duan and I were planning to celebrate midnight out on the ocean. The owner of a fisherman's boat had promised to take us out to sea so we could lie back and gaze at the stars.

I watched Duan pace further off, then turned to look at the waves as their crests appeared on the surface.

Nearby, a boy with a buzz cut was walking in a circle, his face turned toward the sand.

I strolled over to him, thinking I could strike up a conversation and kill some time.

"What are you doing, kid?"

The boy didn't bother to look up. He continued his relentless circles.

"Looking for something."

"Did you lose something, kid? What is it? Do you want me to help you look?" I gazed at the crown of the little boy's head, finding it endearing. Children's crowns always seemed somehow precious to me, while those of adults were strangely pathetic.

The boy didn't answer. His concentration remained glued to the surface of the beach.

"Did you lose it here?" He nodded.

"What is it? So I can help you look."

He raised his right hand and pinched his thumb and index finger together, forming a single tip; his lips were still sealed tight.

I could only guess that the object was diminutive. I began to sweep the ground with my gaze. Near my left foot was a soda cap, concealed among the grains of sand. I bent down to pick it up.

"Is this it?" The boy tilted his head up and looked at the object in my hand for a millisecond before shaking his head.

No other foreign object was in the vicinity.

—

Is the world going to end tomorrow? It doesn't appear so. It would be odd if it blew up into smithereens all of a sudden. Sorn said:

The world isn't going to end. The farangs are being insane. It's just superstitious nonsense, whatever prophesy the religious fanatics believe. In the course of history, who knows how many times deranged people have predicted that the world was going to end, and it hasn't ended yet. But if it does, so be it; it might even be beautiful.

But come to think of it, it probably wouldn't be too good. There's still so many things I want to do. I want to travel around the world. I want to go to Europe. I want to go to the U.S. I want to go China. Especially China. I want to bless my eyes with the sight of the Great Wall, just once in my life. All the Wonders of the World, I want to see them all. I want to see the pyramids. And India. And Nepal.

I want to go stand somewhere elevated; it doesn't matter how far above the sea. Somewhere where my ears would go numb, my legs would stiffen, my heart would beat like the engine of a train as it pulls into the platform, slow but deliberate, rhythmic but purposeful.

A place that can make my eyes sting and tear, but where the liquid that wells up infuses the image before me with a dream-like quality.

I want to look down at the earth, and not rub elbows with it any longer.

I want to be above the world, higher than the reach of life's banality, higher than the cyclical chaos that follows the trajectory of traffic, higher than skyscrapers, higher than democracy, higher than the calories in a chocolate bar, higher than Einstein's IQ, higher than the cost of living in developed countries.

In a place that hasn't been developed and doesn't want to be.

A place where I'll be cold, but where at least I'll know that I'm cold, without having to rely on anyone else's opinion.

I won't have to find out from the Government Spokesperson's announcement. I won't have to listen to the Weather Authority's forecast. My senses won't have to be awakened by department store sales on sweaters and jackets.

A place where I'll know it's cold without relying on language.

A place where I'll know we're cold because my bones tell me so.

If I don't believe in my bones, how could I go on standing?

There in that place, I'd keep standing until my life is no more.

Until my life is no more.

If the world snatched the chance to end first, how could I get to go to such a place? Sorn said:

The world's not going to end tomorrow. Don't worry.

That's what I think, too.

Where did that fisherman disappear to? He promised he'd be waiting for us. If we can't find him, there goes our chance to go star-gazing out on the open sea. We'll have to come up with another plan for our New Year's celebration. Sorn would probably be disappointed. We had our hearts set on listening to the sound of the waves, just the two of us. Hmm, but with the fisherman, that would make three.

Mr. Fisherman, oh, where are you? It's almost sundown.

—

"If you don't tell me what you're looking for, I can't help you look."

The boy was still keeping mum.

"Is it a toy?" I persisted.

The boy shook his head. He furrowed his eyebrows, bringing them close together. I stopped staring down at the sand. The light was beginning to dim. In the dark blue sky, the faint white outline of the moon appeared.

The beachside road was lined with buildings, from low structures to high-rise condominiums, from one-star to two-, three- and four-star hotels. Each establishment was preparing for the night's celebration, to send off the old year and welcome the new. A barrage of fireworks would explode in the sky. Hundreds of paper lanterns would float up, enough to compete with the stars. Even though people on the beach were still preoccupied with their own or family activities, there was no one who didn't feel the approach of the crucial second.

Or perhaps this small child didn't?

"Do you know what tomorrow is, kid?" I asked, becoming genuinely interested in guessing what he was searching for.

The boy regarded me seriously for the first time.

"Of course." His voice showed a hint of aggravation, as if to say, I may be a child, but I'm not altogether clueless – how could he not know the significance of tomorrow?

"What is it, then?" I kept teasing him, being annoying on purpose.

"New Year's." The boy went back to examining the sand.

"And do you know how this New Year's is more special than other New Year's?"

He paused to think for a moment.

"The world's gonna end," he said with confidence.

I laughed in my throat, as an indication that I found his answer cute.

"Is that what you believe? That the world's going to end?"

The boy nodded in earnest.

"And doesn't it scare you?"

He shook his head even more earnestly than he had nodded.

"Why not?"

"Why should I be scared?" The boy crouched down close to the sand. His right hand dug into the fine grains, created by centuries of erosion on the part of the ocean's water. He used all five fingers to squeeze and knead the sand for a while, and then he flung it aside. His little child's hands were still empty. No object had been found.

"Well, wouldn't it be scary if the world ends? Everyone would die. Your parents would die. I'd die. You yourself would die. It's scary."

"Ugh…" The boy exclaimed, visibly annoyed. He stood straight up again and rubbed his palms together, brushing off the sand that clung to the skin.

"…dying is just the blink of an eye."

From a distance, Duan waved to me. Next to her, I could make out the figure of the fisherman who was to take us out to sea on his boat that night.

To die.

In the blink of an eye.

TRANSLATOR'S AFTERWORD

In 2002, you couldn't be Thai and call yourself a reader without knowing the name Prabda Yoon. Having just won the S.E.A. Write Award for *Kwam Na Ja Pen* (the collection from which most of the stories here have been taken), the author was being hailed as the voice of a new generation, of those Thais whose collective consciousness is tied to the experience of growing up in a fast-urbanising country.

Prabda and I are both children of '80s Bangkok, old enough to remember the city without a sky train or a McDonald's, but young enough for these signs of modernisation not to seem out of place when we imagine our hometown. The '80s and '90s were comparatively light-hearted decades in Thailand, with economic realities becoming easier and, for better or worse, politics regarded with relative apathy.

Rapid modernisation paved the way for both hyper-nostalgia and hyper-curiosity about the new, and Prabda captures both of these impulses through his youthful narrators, who often recall their childhoods. The historical moment gave the author his perfect setup: the lightness of the national mood made experimentation in form possible, as the need to convey ideological messages faded into the background. Meanwhile, the lives of many Thais were moving further and further away from the rice paddies romanticised in much of the existing literature.

Prabda's arrival – and his influence – ushered in an era of Thai literature that broke away from realism. His stories demand to be perceived as texts, insisting on their own self-contained universes made up of words and letters. Punctuation takes on a life of its own, despite its usage being relatively rare in Thai (and mostly imported). Wordplay is another of Prabda's trademarks, drawing attention to the fact that any given language is a game with its own internal logic – a challenge for the translator, who attempts to recreate his moves in a language where the rules are different.

For example, Prabda plays with the fact that Thai does not generally use spaces between words. Meanings can therefore multiply because there are instances where two words next to each other have independent meanings on their own, while also forming a compound whose meaning can be completely unrelated to those of its component words. There is มดเท็จ ("mod-tej") in "Pen in Parentheses," for instance: as a whole, it means "to lie," but มด ("mod") alone means "ant" (symbolising smallness in Thai) and เท็จ ("tej") means "false." I turned these ants into bees in the translation, to keep the word game that the narrator relies on for his absurd line of reasoning.

Prabda also has fun with Thai names, particularly nicknames, which often have immediately apparent meanings. Many of them will seem silly to non-Thais – Duck, Melon, and Rat are perfectly normal nicknames. In "A Schoolgirl's Diary," two of the teachers are called "Moo" (meaning "Pig"); another is called "Mod" (the same word for "ant" again) so the kids nickname her "Mod X," the Thai title of the Japanese manga series "Kamen Rider X." In rendering the humour here, I had to break the usual rule of not translating or changing names.

I hope I have done Prabda's wit sufficient justice, so that readers of the translation will get a good taste of his style. I also hope that the Bangkok obliquely represented in these stories will come alive for the reader as it does for me, as the city of those days is the one I always come home to.

This edition first published in the United Kingdom by Tilted Axis Press in 2017.

tiltedaxispress.com

First published in Thai as ความน่าจะเป็น (*Kwam Na Ja Pen*) by Amarin Printing and Publishing Public Company Limited in 2000.

'Found' and 'Marut by the Sea' were first published in Two Lines, 'Pen in Parentheses' in Asymptote, and 'Ei Ploang' in Words without Borders.

ISBN (paperback)   9781911284062
ISBN (ebook)   9781911284079

A catalogue record for this book is available from the British Library.

Edited by Deborah Smith
Typesetting and ebook production by Simon Collinson
Printed and bound by CPI Group (UK) Ltd, Croydon, CR0 4YY

This book has been selected to receive financial assistance from English PEN's "PEN Translates!" programme, supported by Arts Council England. English PEN exists to promote literature and our understanding of it, to uphold writers' freedoms around the world, to campaign against the persecution and imprisonment of writers for stating their views, and to promote the friendly co-operation of writers and the free exchange of ideas. www.englishpen.org

ABOUT TILTED AXIS PRESS

Founded in 2015 and based in Sheffield and London, Tilted Axis is a not-for-profit press on a mission to shake up contemporary international literature.

Tilted Axis publishes the books that might not otherwise make it into English, for the very reasons that make them exciting to us — artistic originality, radical vision, the sense that here is something new.

Tilting the axis of world literature from the centre to the margins allows us to challenge that very division. These margins are spaces of compelling innovation, where multiple traditions spark new forms and translation plays a crucial role.

As part of carving out a new direction in the publishing industry, Tilted Axis is also dedicated to improving access. We're proud to pay our translators the proper rate, and to operate without unpaid interns.

We hope you find this fantastic book as thrilling and beguiling as we do, and if you do, we'd love to know.

tiltedaxispress.com
@TiltedAxisPress